Could she trust Captain Grant? She didn't like him, because he hadn't wanted to help her. He made her feel like an unpleasant obstacle that he would deal with only to get her out of the way quickly.

Her doubts surged back to thoughts about her new family's reaction to her. How could they possibly love her after eighteen years? ... Would strangers accept someone reared by the feared and hated Comanche? She felt safe and secure with the Tatums. Why couldn't she stay? Yet even as she asked herself these questions she knew she would go. Her curiosity was as strong as her desire for a family.

Additional Meadowsong Romances—action-packed and heart-stirring, they capture the spirit of the untamed western prairies of the late 1800s:

From Barbara Masci	*From Irene Brand*
Forbidden Legacy	Freedom's Call
Captured Heart	The Touchstone

BY Barbara A. Masci:

Captured Heart

Forbidden Legacy

Stolen Heritage

STOLEN HERITAGE

BARBARA A·MASCI

Fleming H. Revell Company
Old Tappan, New Jersey

Scripture quotations in this volume are from the King James Version of the Bible.

Library of Congress Cataloging-in-Publication Data

Masci, Barbara.
Stolen heritage / Barbara A. Masci.
p. cm.
ISBN 0-8007-5369-0
1. Comanche Indians—Captivities—Fiction. I. Title.
PS3563.A7817S7 1990
813'.54—dc20

90-8498
CIP

Published by the Fleming H. Revell Company
Old Tappan, New Jersey 07675
Printed in the United States of America

STOLEN HERITAGE

Prologue
June 19, 1854

Brushing the damp hair from her face, the woman sighed. Texas heat certainly beat anything she'd ever felt back East. Stooping, she picked another piece of laundry from her bucket and shook it before hanging it over the rope strung between the house and the large cottonwood tree.

An auburn-haired baby fussed from atop the blanket spread beneath the shade tree. The mother clucked in the baby's direction and continued tending to the clothes. "Just let me finish with this laundry, and I'll pick you up," she promised, hanging the last shirt. "And when your father comes home, we'll have a nice supper!"

"There." She stooped to pick up her daughter. Kissing the infant's cheek, she walked toward the house. As a cluster of birds flew off noisily from a tree in front of the house she stopped short, wondering, *Now what stirred them?*

With a shrug, she turned back toward the house, only to halt again with a gasp. A wildly painted Indian blocked her path. Quickly she turned to flee, but several other savages surrounded her. The various colors that striped their faces made them grotesque and frightening. The woman struggled and screamed as the bronzed, bare-chested men grabbed her.

Instinctively, she clutched her eight-month-old baby more tightly. The sneering faces nearly touched hers, and their mouths shouted words she did not understand.

Without warning, one Indian yanked the child from her arms. The last thing the woman heard was her daughter's screaming; then she felt a red-hot, searing pain in her forehead, before darkness enveloped her entire being.

1

April, 1872

The lovely young woman rested her fair-complected cheek against the window sill and sighed. Her auburn braid fell over one thin, but muscular shoulder and turned a glittering red by the strong sun's ray. Running Brook yawned and flipped the heavy braid back over her shoulder and stretched lazily. She wondered if she'd ever be able to sleep without being abruptly awakened by horrid nightmares. Would visions of marauding Indian warriors carrying bloody scalps always haunt her dreams? She prayed daily that the nightmares of snakes, gory deaths, and taunting Indian children would disappear. She had a new life now. Why did the horrid memories linger in her subconscious?

Standing, she straightened her white buckskin dress and stretched her toes, pushing them roughly into white ankle-high moccasins. Cocking her head to one side, she listened intently. Then throwing her waist-length, auburn braid over her shoulder, she tiptoed noiselessly to the bedroom door. A strange voice rang through the small cottage.

Opening the door slightly, she pressed her ear against the slit. Her door's position at the top of the stairs enabled her to hear clearly, yet Running Brook didn't bother to peek out, for it was impossible to see anyone below. She listened carefully, stiffened at the mention of her name, and opened the door a bit wider.

"You'd better start at the beginning, Mr. Tatum." The deep voice drifted up the stairs. "You've lost me. What have I to do with a girl you found with the Comanche? Why did you call me?"

"Sorry, Captain Grant, but I'd thought everyone around here knew about Running Brook and her dilemma." This was Mr. Tatum, the Indian agent who had so kindly taken Running Brook in two years ago.

The strange voice offered, "I did hear something about you taking in an Indian or something."

"Not an Indian," Mr. Tatum corrected emphatically. "A white woman who'd been kidnapped from her cradle over sixteen years before."

"A white woman? Sixteen years?" he asked.

"Well," Mr. Lawrie Tatum said, "it was the talk of the area once. Thank the Lord the gossip has settled down, for too many false stories circulated about this affair. I'll give you the truth. Will you have coffee?"

Running Brook heard dishes clattering and knew Mrs. Tatum had served coffee and biscuits. After the initial noise of the serving had passed, Mr. Tatum told the army captain, "Two years ago another Comanche tribe surrendered to the reservation, due to starvation. Red Warrior, the chief, confessed his tribe had a white captive. The way he told it, he'd given a war trophy of a baby girl to his son, Big Bear, and his barren first wife.

"This child, known only as Running Brook, was around sixteen years old when she came to us. Not knowing what else to do with her, my wife and I took her in. She was quite primitive then, but we've educated her in the social graces, hoping she might one day fit into society."

The large, bald-headed man added in a reminiscent tone, "Seems like yesterday, but that was the winter of 1870, and here we are in the spring of seventy-two. In all that time we've only just finished sifting through the information we received from the government. When we asked, they sent us a list of families from that specific area who'd lost infant daughters around the time Red Warrior said they'd captured her. We've acted discreetly, not wanting to harm this lovely girl's reputation and future—people are very critical toward women who've been with Indians. By quietly checking government records and comparing them with the meager information Red Warrior supplied, we have come up with two families."

Agent Tatum stopped and cleared his throat. "I don't have the time to investigate them further," he explained. "That's why I called you."

"Me, an army captain, investigating a missing person? What do you expect me to do?" the soldier asked.

Running Brook could picture Mr. Tatum leaning back in his chair, with his arms across his chest, as he usually did when he talked seriously.

"Captain Grant, I called you because I'm a good Quaker, a man of God, and I've heard you are a good servant of God also. Though you aren't a Friend, I've heard excellent reports of your ministry among the soldiers. Mrs. Tatum and I feel we can trust you. We've become fond of Running Brook and feel she is entitled to the life from which the Indians snatched her. Will you help us?"

The stranger's voice, while calm, held the merest edge of irritation. "Mr. Tatum, I'm a soldier, not a detective. What would you have me do? Isn't there someone more suited you could call?"

"Colonel Grierson thought you'd be anxious to help . . . ," Mr. Tatum murmured.

"The colonel!" Captain Grant gasped. "You spoke to the colonel about this?"

"Of course. Actually, it was he who first mentioned you. Since the army is directly responsible for the return of Indian captives, this is his concern. He recommended you highly and even promised you an indefinite leave of absence until the matter was completely settled."

Running Brook opened the door a crack wider, for she heard no response. She hoped she hadn't missed it.

"Then," the captain began, "this isn't exactly a voluntary job, is it?"

"We all thought you best for the mission" was all Tatum said.

"Where do I begin?" the captain asked with a sigh.

"The government supplied me with names, many of which I've been able to eliminate because of the location or incorrect age of the child. As I said, I've narrowed it down to two families. It shouldn't be too difficult or time consuming to determine which family the girl belongs to. However, I cannot stress enough the importance of using discretion."

"You want me to simply call on these families and interrogate them?" the captain asked.

"Yes, but with the girl. She will leave with you."

"With me?" he protested. "How can a young woman travel with me alone? If you think living with the Indians gave her a bad name, wait until—"

"No, Grant, we've thought of that. The colonel said you had a mother living in Fort Worth. We'll wait until you bring her back with you. The families you'll be visiting are both in Fort Worth. Another reason we chose you."

"Mr. Tatum, my mother is sixty years old. I'll not subject her to a trip all the way from Fort Worth and back. Have you no one who can go with us?"

"No one," Tatum answered firmly.

"My mother is *not* traveling," the captain stated without hesitation.

"I understand," Tatum said kindly. "I'll think of something. How soon can you be ready to leave?"

"The sooner the better. I'm anxious to get this over with."

"Excellent. Running Brook will be ready the day after tomorrow."

Running Brook silently closed the door when she heard the captain and Mr. Tatum saying farewells. Sitting upon her overstuffed sofa, she contemplated the conversation. Mr. Tatum had located two families, one of them hers, but what had the Indian agent meant when he'd said, "People are very critical toward women who've been with Indians"?

A soft knock on her door brought Running Brook abruptly from her thoughts. At her invitation Mr. and Mrs. Lawrie Tatum entered her room and sat down upon the two upright chairs facing her sofa.

"Hello, my dear," greeted the balding and bearded Indian agent. "How is the headache?"

"Gone. I took a nap," she replied with a smile. These people had been good to her. They'd taught her white ways and shown her God's love. She liked them. "I'm sorry I didn't finish helping you make jam," she directed toward Mrs. Tatum.

Mrs. Tatum smiled with her eyes as well as her lips. "Pay it no mind, dear. There is plenty more for tomorrow, if you feel up to it."

"Well," Mr. Tatum said abruptly. "To get to the point of our visit, we have good news."

Mrs. Tatum patted Running Brook's arm. "Good news for you, but not us, I'm afraid."

"Let me tell it, dear," Mr. Tatum said with a touch of impatience. "Running Brook, you are finally going home."

Running Brook hesitated long enough so they wouldn't suspect she'd heard the whole conversation, then asked, "Home? What do you mean?"

She watched the portly Quaker lean back in his chair and cross his arms over his chest. "We've been investigating throughout the last year or so and have come up with two families that could be yours. Captain Jeremy Grant and his scout from Fort Sill will accompany you to his home in Fort Worth, where you will be his guest until he can determine which family you belong to. I've heard his mother is a charming woman and superb hostess."

"I see," she said. "Do I travel alone with these men?"

"Ah-h, that's one of our problems," Tatum said, sitting straight. "But Mrs. Tatum has an idea." He nodded at his wife, his consent for her to speak.

"I will dress you up as a lad. That way no one will know you travel in the company of two men. No one has a bad word to say of either man, and I trust both of them completely, but you know how gossip is. We must protect your reputation. When you get to Fort Worth, Mrs. Grant will supply you with clothes, and you can make your debut as . . . ," she faltered.

"Who?" Running Brook asked, "Who am I?"

"I can give you two possibilities," offered Mr. Tatum. "You are either the daughter of Angus McCallister or Elmer Garrison. Both are prominent men from Fort Worth."

"McCallister? Garrison?" she asked, sounding the names carefully.

"Both lost daughters to Indian raids around eighteen

years ago." Mr. Tatum stood, and Mrs. Tatum followed his lead. They walked toward the door.

"You're a very fortunate young woman. Both families are respected, well-to-do families. You can't go wrong with either. Be sure to thank the good Lord. Oh, and you leave day after tomorrow."

Before Running Brook could ask one of the many questions that darted into her mind, they had disappeared from her room. She plopped herself upon her bed. *Was* she fortunate? Would her family welcome her with open arms? Did she have a mother other than Yellow Moon? A father who would beat her the way Big Bear had? Or would he be kind, like her friend Singing Bird's father?

Running Brook sighed. She would miss Yellow Moon, who still visited her often. Though she was not her real mother, Running Brook loved the woman dutifully. After all, Yellow Moon was the only mother she'd known—yet the memories of things she had done still frightened Running Brook and cooled warmer feelings for the barren Indian woman.

Who was the other man she would travel with? Could she trust Captain Grant? She didn't like him, because he hadn't wanted to help her. He made her feel like an unpleasant obstacle that he would deal with only to get her out of the way quickly.

Her doubts surged back to thoughts about her new family's reaction toward her. How could they possibly love her after eighteen years? Mrs. Tatum said they guessed she had been close to a year old when she'd been taken captive. Would strangers accept someone reared by the feared and hated Comanche? She felt safe and secure with the Tatums. Why couldn't she stay? Yet even as she asked herself these questions she knew she would go. Her curiosity was as strong as her desire for a family.

* * *

Three travelers on horseback pulled fresh mounts behind them. From Fort Sill to Tent City—a town named by the Wichita Indians—they passed not one house or other sign of civilization.

Running Brook remained silent for the first few days, studying the two young men who accompanied her. Captain Grant, a tall, thin, clean-shaven young man, reinforced Running Brook's initial opinion of him: cold and heartless, he seemed anxious to do his duty and be rid of her. Her only concession in his favor was that he had pleasing features; she especially liked his large, warm, brown eyes.

The Indian scout, an educated Kiowa, wore a uniform similar to the captain's. His name was Trail Dust, which Captain Grant had shortened to Dusty. Short, stocky, and always ready with a smile, the scout didn't frighten Running Brook, as many Indian men did. She reasoned it was probably because he reminded her of Little Fox, her Indian cousin. Little Fox and Singing Bird had been her best playmates while growing up. Despite the many horrid memories of her life with the Comanche, whenever she thought of her two dear friends, she almost yearned to return.

Before they left, Mr. Tatum had supplied Running Brook with brown breeches, cinched with a rope belt, and a yellow flannel shirt. Her hair was stuffed beneath a large, floppy felt hat. She didn't resent being dressed as a lad: The clothes were comfortable and perfect for traveling.

At night they placed their bedrolls beside the fire, and two slept while one watched. Halfway through the night, they switched guards. Spared that chore, Running Brook slept the night through.

Early on the third night, Running Brook and Dusty slumbered while Captain Grant kept watch. She felt especially tired, having slept lightly the first two nights. As she floated into dark timelessness, her recurrent dreams invaded her rest. Dead babies flashed before her; braves held bloody scalps; and she relived the brutal beatings from her Indian father.

A shrill scream woke her. Finding herself in a sitting position, Running Brook realized the cry had been her own. Still shaken from the nightmare, she began to weep softly, only to scream again when a hand grasped her shoulder from behind.

2

"Don't touch me!" she gasped, then closed her eyes in relief. It was only Captain Grant.

Quickly removing his hand, he showed the first sign of compassion she'd seen. "What happened? Did something frighten you?"

Running Brook fearfully stared up into his concerned eyes and breathed in quick gasps. She gulped. "Why did you touch me?"

"I'm sorry. I don't know, except I was worried." His cold, heartless expression returned. "I'm not used to women screaming out in Indian territory in the middle of the night, I guess."

Her face whitened at his words. "In-Indian territory?"

"But that shouldn't bother you. You lived with them. Maybe I should be the one. . . . Hey, you're shaking. You really *are* afraid!" He reached out to touch her trembling arm, then drew back quickly. "You okay?"

"Why are you so cruel?" she blurted.

"Cruel? Me? Never."

"Insensitive then." The first word came out a syllable at a time.

"Maybe."

"Why?"

He shrugged, looking away.

"Because you didn't want the job of helping me?"

"Don't take it personally."

"Then try to understand," she said, "how difficult this is for me."

He looked at her carefully. Shaking his head, he offered, "I didn't mean to offend you. I would have been glad to help if only. . . ."

She cocked her head, making her braid fall over one shoulder. "If only. . . ."

He sighed. "If only it weren't *now*."

She noticed the pain in his brown eyes and wondered if she should ask what caused it.

"Why did you scream?" he asked.

"Bad dreams."

"Like what?" he asked.

"Like some things I experienced while living with the Comanche."

"It never occurred to me that you were unhappy with the Indians. After all, you were brought up from infancy with them."

She studied him carefully before replying, "You would think so, wouldn't you? Yet you have no idea what I have seen."

"But you were one of them," he protested.

"Was I?" she asked with one eyebrow raised. *Why does this man think he knows me and my life?* she wondered.

"You were just an infant when the Comanche took you. Didn't you think, at first, you were one of them?"

"Never," she stated positively.

"Want to talk about it?" he asked.

"No!" she snapped. Why would he think she'd confide in him? She could trust no one with her private life.

He shrugged, then said simply, "If you're all right, I'll let you get back to sleep. If you need me, call."

"Thank you," she whispered to his retreating back.

As she curled beneath her bedroll Running Brook asked herself how that cold, heartless man could now seem so sensitive and kind. Perhaps it was just an act. She'd watch him. How else could she tell if he could be trusted?

At least, she reasoned, gazing at the stars, *now we're on good terms. It will make this trip more comfortable.* She'd make a point to get to know Dusty better, too, she promised herself as she drifted to sleep.

As they traveled the next day she pondered on why this trip came at a bad time for Captain Grant. Should she have asked why? No, she reasoned. Hadn't she just mentally scolded him for prying into her personal life? It was not her business.

When they made camp that night, she helped Dusty prepare supper while the captain tended the horses. Dusty had caught several large fish from a stream, and Running Brook had cleaned them. They sat before the fire, inhaling the sweet aroma of the browning fish.

"Hm-m, sure smells good," Running Brook remarked casually. "Aren't they done yet?"

"We don't want to rush them," Dusty said. "The longer they roast, the better they taste."

"Not always," she remarked. "Remember the first night you made fish? Downright burnt they were."

"Burnt! They were perfect."

"Were not! They were burnt. Even Captain Grant said they were a touch dark."

"*Dark*, but not *black!*"

"Pretty close."

"Would you like to cook them, then?" he asked.

Running Brook smiled. "Then they'd probably be half raw, because you know how anxious I always am to eat."

Dusty laughed, then sobered. "Can I ask you a question?"

"I guess so."

"You have nightmares and seem so unhappy. Was your life with the Comanche so terrible?"

She hesitated, reluctant to disclose her life to yet another stranger. How should she answer? How much should she tell?

"The Indians weren't so terrible; crude, maybe, but not so horrid. It was just my misfortune to be adopted by a troubled family."

Dusty nodded sympathetically, inspiring her to continue, despite her vow not to say too much. "Why the bad dreams, then?"

"There were things I saw, gruesome things, that are a part of the Comanche everyday life. They had no idea the effect it would have on me. Most were loving, friendly people. If only I'd had parents like Singing Bird's."

"Singing Bird?" he repeated. "Tell me about Singing Bird."

Thrown off guard by his interest, she told him about her friend.

"She is beautiful and warmhearted. Singing Bird was close to my age and my dearest, trusted friend. Her parents were wonderful, too."

"Unlike yours?" he prompted.

"I'm sure that fish is done now."

He smiled. "Okay, so you don't wish to discuss it. I understand. Thank you for sharing so much with me."

Why had she told him so much? Running Brook felt strangely at home with Dusty. Could it be because he was Indian? *Was* she more Indian than she thought?

With a long twig, Running Brook tried to spear one of the fish over the fire. Dusty tried to shield the fish with his arm. "They aren't done!"

"Mine is," she said, trying again to spear one.

"Is not," Dusty contended, trying to take the stick from her.

"Is too," she teased, dodging his efforts.

Grabbing her hand, he tried to twist the stick from her grasp. Laughing, she tried to wriggle her hand from his.

A deep voice broke into their fun and brought them both to attention. "I hope I'm not disturbing you two. I could go back to the horses and return later. However, I *am* hungry."

Running Brook blushed, though she knew not why. She'd not done anything wrong. Why was Captain Grant scowling at them? What made her feel ashamed?

Dusty spoke first. "Don't be silly, Captain. It was only horseplay. Running Brook was trying to steal herself a fish before it was ready. Looks done now. Let's eat."

Still frowning, the captain joined them for supper.

While Running Brook did not fully trust either man, she felt no danger from them, especially Dusty. However, after several days of disapproving glares from Captain Grant, the nightmares resumed.

The first two nights Dusty ran to her side and comforted her. But the third night the tired Kiowa slept soundly, and Captain Grant knelt over her as she trembled and sobbed.

He didn't touch her but merely asked softly if she were all right. When she nodded tearfully, he asked, "Were you dreaming of an animal chasing you? Is that the problem?"

She cocked her head at him in puzzlement. "Animal?"

"Yes." He explained, "You called out something about a big bear."

"Oh!" she gasped. Smiling slightly, she said simply, "It's not an animal, but an Indian named Big Bear."

"Ah," he said. "I remember. Big Bear was your Indian father, the chief's son."

"Yes. Father," she answered sourly.

"And you didn't care for him I take it."

She shook her head. "I hated him!"

"Now, now," he clucked. "Hate is mighty strong. We aren't supposed to hate."

Running Brook's eyes widened, and her cheeks grew red. "Not hate someone who burns and beats you whenever no one can see?"

"Burns? Beats?" Captain Grant repeated. "Is this part of your dream? A fantasy?"

Running Brook clenched her teeth and searched for the correct words. Failing, she ripped at the button of her shirt cuff and yanked up her sleeve. "Look," was all she said.

"Dear God," he murmured, staring in horror at the large, puckered scars. "Big Bear did this?"

She nodded, pulling her sleeve down.

His eyes filled with such compassion that she almost didn't react to his pat on the hand. "You poor . . . ," he began, until she withdrew her hand like a flash. "Sorry. I didn't mean to touch you." He turned, then said over his shoulder, "Though you don't seem to mind *Dusty* touching you."

The next evening, after supper, Running Brook approached Captain Grant as he sipped coffee beside the fire. "May I have a word with you, sir?" she asked boldly.

"Of course," he answered, making room for her beside him on the ground. "How may I be of service?"

"Mr. Tatum said there were two families I might belong

to. I've forgotten the names. Could you tell me anything about them?"

"My word!" he exclaimed. Setting his cup down, he searched his pockets. "I'd forgotten to look at the names myself. I must know both. I know everyone for miles around Fort Worth." Discovering the folded envelope in his back pocket, he opened it impatiently. He scanned the paper within and gasped. "McCallister! I don't believe it! Garrison perhaps, but not McCallister!" At the sight of her large, curious eyes, he explained, "Not that they aren't distinguished, well-to-do men, it's just that—" he broke off, shaking his head. "I'm just shocked that the McCallister family should, after all these years, come into my life in so many ways *now*."

"I don't understand," she said, recognizing the same inflection on the word *now* as he had used when speaking of this ill-timed trip.

"Oh! Sorry." He spoke as if he'd forgotten she was there.

"Can you tell me anything about these families?" she asked.

"Yes, I suppose I can," he said. "They are both good ones. The McCallisters have a son, but I think Mrs. McCallister is Angus's second wife, and I believe the son, Ramsey, is hers from a previous marriage. I'm really not sure. Like I said, our lives hardly ever touched before. I've never been close to either family; I only know who they are."

"The Garrisons are Elmer and. . . ." Captain Grant scratched his head. "Can't recall Mrs. Garrison's first name. *Margaret, Martha,* or something. They had no children, except the infant who was kidnapped by the Comanche."

"Which do you think is my family?"

"I can only hope it's the Garrisons."

"Why do you say that?"

He studied her for several moments before answering.

"It's nothing against old Angus himself, mind you, but another McCallister family member and I are sure to have problems."

Running Brook cocked her head to one side. "I don't understand."

Captain Grant stood, brushed off his pant legs and said, "That's all I can tell you, Brook." Before she could react to her new abbreviated name, he had vanished.

As she lay under the stars, bundled against the chilly Texas night, she replayed the conversation over and over in her mind. He hadn't revealed much about her family, and his remarks about the McCallisters had her puzzled. But *Brook,* he'd called her. She liked that. *Brook.* She smiled and snuggled deeper into her bedroll.

As she listened to the night wilderness sounds, she shivered, despite lying so close to the fire. The Indian women never seemed to mind the frightful night sounds, but she'd always cringed. Her fear had made her a prime target for scary stories. The boys had always made great fun of coming up behind her at night and making noises or grabbing her to make her scream. Yet she'd never gotten used to it. The dark nights, with eerie animal calls and shadowy forms, still unnerved her. She huddled deeper within her blanket.

Dusty turned from his bedroll nearby.

"You okay?" he whispered.

She turned toward him. "Sure. Just cold."

He got out of his bed, carelessly searched through his pack, then walked over to her with a woolen cape and placed it over her blanket. "Don't have another blanket, but this poncho will help."

"Thank you, Dusty," she said fondly.

He started to walk away.

"Dusty!" she called softly.

He stopped, turned, and knelt down on one knee. "Yeah?"

"Why are you so good to me?" she asked innocently.

He smiled. "I like you. . . ." He hesitated. "And because I feel I must prove to you that all Indians are not like the ones who mistreated you."

"I know that."

"Good." He winked, patting her hand.

She looked up at him, smiling.

"Excuse me!" A deep voice from the darkness made them both jump. "Aren't you going to get any sleep, Dusty? You'll be plenty tired, come time for your watch."

"Yes, Captain. I was just saying good-night." Dusty waved to Running Brook as he headed back to his own bedroll.

Captain Grant scowled at Running Brook. "You'd best get some sleep; it'll be another long day tomorrow."

"Good night, Captain Grant," she responded stiffly. Though she turned her back toward him, she could feel his eyes on her for several minutes before she heard him walk away.

The next morning Brook washed in a creek sprouting from the Trinity River. Gazing into the distance, beyond where Dusty and Captain Grant saddled the horses, she felt anxious to begin. For today they neared their destination; this could be their last full day on the trail.

Patting her face dry with the long linen cloth Mrs. Tatum had packed for her, she felt something jump at her and attach itself to the cloth. Brook leaped up, screamed as she never had before, and threw the cloth as far from her as she could.

Numbly, she heard the men running toward her, but she shrieked again as the discarded cloth moved stealthily toward her.

3

The cloth crept closer to Brook, and her cries grew shriller. Captain Grant, coming up behind her, took the situation in hand. Leaning over, he cautiously removed the linen from the slithering form. Brook gasped, then stared incredibly at the intruder. With unshed tears still glowing in her bright-blue eyes, she smiled and dropped to her knees.

The captain stood with hands on hips and smirked. "Your attacker, m'lady."

Brook shot him a piercing look, then called to Dusty. "Look, it's a kitten! Where do you suppose it came from?" She gently picked up the gray bundle of fluff and stroked it lovingly.

Grant had already begun to search the area nearby, and Brook saw him kneel down and pull something out of the water a few hundred feet upstream. Dusty ran to his side. Brook stood where she'd found her kitten, hugging it to her, when she noticed the two men seemed unusually concerned about what they had found.

"What's wrong?" she called.

"Nothing. Stay there," Captain Grant ordered.

Clutching the kitten tightly to her chest, she ran to them. "What is it?" she asked, then gasped in shock for the second time that morning.

"Is it alive?" she whispered.

"Barely," Grant said.

Looking down at the bloody larger cat, Brook asked, "What happened to it?"

"Got caught in a trap," Dusty said. "I think it's the kitten's mother."

Unaware of its mother's peril, the kitten purred loudly in Brook's arms. She kissed its head. "Can you save her?"

"Take your kitten and go back to the horses and stay there," Captain Grant ordered.

"B-but—"

Captain Grant snapped angrily. "Take her away, Dusty."

"Yes, sir. C'mon, Brook. Hurry."

They had barely reached the horses when a gunshot thundered through the quiet morning air. The kitten's claws dug into her arm in fright. Brook spun around to face Dusty. "He shot her!"

He shrugged helplessly.

"Why did he kill her?"

"I guess," Dusty fumbled for the words, "I guess she was wounded too badly to save."

"I was right about him. Only a cold, heartless man could kill a helpless mother cat without hesitation."

"Listen, Brook—" Dusty began.

But Captain Grant walked briskly up to them and distracted Dusty from what he was about to say.

Strapping his shotgun to his saddle, Grant said without emotion, "Dusty, please bury her while I look around for more kittens."

Dusty ran off in the direction of the cat, and Captain Grant began to scour the brush, whisking the growth about, so he could see beneath. As Brook watched him search she wondered if she'd misjudged Captain Grant. Would a cold, heartless man comb the fields for orphaned kittens?

No more kittens were found, but Brook secretly thought Captain Grant a better man, because he searched diligently for almost an hour.

They neared Fort Worth the next afternoon. Captain Grant ordered that Dusty and Brook remain at a distance until dark, to protect Running Brook's reputation. Meanwhile he went ahead to announce their coming to his mother, so she could ready things for their arrival. With Brook's permission, the captain took Smoky, her kitten, with him. He promised the animal would be well cared for until she could join him.

Running Brook and Dusty walked along a rocky ridge outside Fort Worth. She gazed at the city. "Dusty! It's bigger than I'd imagined. I'll surely get lost wandering about. The buildings all look so similar. How will I learn my way around?"

"It's easy. You'll learn," he answered. "Can you read?"

"A little. Mrs. Tatum taught me. I've never finished a whole book or anything, but I can read."

"That'll help. You see, all those look-alike buildings have signs on them. Each is a place of business—except the houses, of course, and they have individual touches that tell them apart."

"Oh, but what is that white building with part of the top sticking up high, like a tree?"

"That's a church. Have you never seen a church?" Dusty asked curiously.

"No. What's a church?"

"You mean your Quaker benefactors didn't tell you what a church was?"

"I'm not sure what a *benefactor* is, but the Tatums never mentioned a church, unless I wasn't paying attention."

"A church is a place people go to worship God and have Christian fellowship."

She gave him a knowing look. "You mean a meeting house? Mr. Tatum had one built behind his house."

Dusty nodded. "Yes. Our church building serves as a church, school, and meeting house."

Dusty changed the subject. "Let's sit on that rock, yonder. No one can see us at this distance, and we can look at the town while we talk."

Running Brook sat beside him and gazed at the town in wonder. "I'm fascinated by Fort Worth, yet it frightens me."

"Captain Grant and I wouldn't let any harm come to you," he assured her.

"I know *you* wouldn't, but Captain Grant I'm not so sure of."

"Why?"

"He didn't want the job of escorting me and hasn't made a secret of it."

"Perhaps he has good reason."

"The way he did for shooting Smoky's mother?"

"Something like that. The cat had to be put out of her misery. She was suffering. Captain Grant did her a favor." Dusty sighed. "Nevertheless, he'd not let anything happen to you. I can promise you that. Captain Grant is an honorable man."

Running Brook studied the Indian's face for a clue to his true character. His eyes were small, but his gaze steady. Dusty wore his hair cropped shorter than most Indian men's. His high cheekbones gave him a proud look. His thick lips, which almost always smiled, warmed his words. To her surprise, she found herself trusting him. She'd promised herself never to trust anyone again, especially an Indian man, but Dusty was nothing like Big Bear.

"You're close friends with the captain?" she asked.

"Yes, he's been my benefactor." He smiled and winked kindly. "That means he's been good to me, helped me become what I am today."

"What is good about Captain Grant?" she asked without malice.

"Let me ask you something first. Did the Tatums teach you about God and heaven?"

Running Brook laughed. "Every day, all day!"

Dusty laughed with her, then asked, "What did you think about it?"

"I believe in God, and I pray as they taught me. I'm white, and the Tatums' God is my God, not the Indian—" Her hand flew to her mouth. "I'm sorry—"

But Dusty merely laughed. When he finally stopped, he said, "Don't be sorry. But let me explain something. Your God is for everyone, not just white people."

"But," she began excitedly, "the Comanche never prayed to God or believed in Him! They worship the sun, moon, and earth and pray to the Great Spirit."

"Yes, but didn't Tatum try to teach the reservation Indians about our God?" he asked, still smiling.

"Yes, but few listened. They pretended, just to get on his good side for favors."

"But," Dusty pointed his finger at her, "why would he bother to teach them about a God who wasn't for them, too?"

Running Brook considered his point. "I guess you're right, but God isn't an Indian."

Dusty laughed again. "What difference does that make?"

Running Brook was becoming uncomfortable with this subject and Dusty's laughing at her ignorance. "Why all the questions about God anyway? What does this have to do with the good in Captain Grant?"

"Because Captain Grant is an extremely dedicated Christian man. You never have to fear him; he'd not hurt you or anyone," said Dusty reverently.

"Is he a Quaker, too?" she asked, wide-eyed.

"No. In fact he isn't affiliated with any structured religious group. He just reads his Bible, teaches others, and lives what he believes."

"Does he go to a church?" she asked.

"Yes, whenever he can. He prays and worships at home or on the trail when he cannot."

"How does his being a Christian man mean I can trust him?" she asked.

"Because he believes the Bible, God's words, and lives what they tell him. God's Word tells him to be kind and not to hurt anyone."

"But he *isn't* kind to me. He scowls, and he's angry because he has to escort me and find my family," she said pointedly.

"Even Christians aren't perfect. He is still human and has human emotions that God doesn't have. Earthly pressures get in the way for people and cause us to be less than God."

"So he *could* harm me?" she asked.

"Never. Trust me. He might get angry and touchy sometimes, but harm anyone? Never."

She looked up at him and spoke earnestly. "You're the first person I've truly trusted in a long time."

He smiled and took her hand. "I'm glad. Especially since I'm an Indian." He kissed her hand and winked.

"I hope I'm not intruding." Grant's voice caused them to jump.

Dusty dropped her hand. "Not at all, Captain. I was just showing Running Brook our town. She's never seen a town or a church before. She's quite awestruck."

"She surely appears to be struck by something." He said the words half beneath his breath, yet Dusty and Running Brook clearly heard them and blushed uncomfortably.

Scowling at her, the captain said, "Well, Brook, you'll be pleased to hear my mother is preparing for your arrival. In fact at this moment she is buying you appropriate clothing. I only hope you won't disappoint her."

Running Brook stood. Anger erupted within her at his words. "Disappoint her? How would I do that?"

Captain Grant walked toward her and fingered his riding crop carefully. "My mother is a kind, generous woman. I just want to be sure you appreciate her and her efforts." He shrugged. "I hope you are considerate of her and realize all she is doing to make you welcome."

"Why wouldn't I?" she asked. "Because I grew up with Indians, you think I don't have manners?"

Captain Grant's gaze dropped to the ground in embarrassment. "I'm sorry, I didn't mean—"

"I can assure you, Captain Grant, that Mr. and Mrs. Tatum were never embarrassed by my behavior. I may not have learned social graces from the Comanche, but they did teach me manners. I was taught to respect family and fellow tribesmen. Rules of behavior were drilled into me by many teachers at a very early age." She ended her speech, quickly whirled on her heel, and spun away from the men.

By the light of a mere crescent moon, the three slowly trotted through the dark, seemingly forlorn streets of Fort Worth—up one street and down another, first a right turn, then a left turn. Brook wondered how she could know where she was or where she'd end up. She silently followed

Captain Grant, and Dusty trod behind her. Whenever she felt distressed, she turned to him for support. His wink or smile of assurance kept her spirits up.

Now Brook noted that the buildings they passed appeared to be mostly homes, which progressively grew farther apart. They no longer marched through the heart of the city. Without warning, a large, rotund woman ran from her post behind a white picket-fenced home. She waved frantically and grinned a warm welcome to them all.

When Brook gazed upon the warm brown eyes and rosy-cheeked, wholesome smile, she knew Mrs. Grant would be her friend—despite her feelings for her son, Captain Jeremy Grant. Flora Grant embraced her son as soon as he leaped from his horse. Then she ran to Brook and helped her dismount, hugging her with true affection.

"Welcome home, my dear," the woman greeted Running Brook, patting her back lovingly. "My home is your home. You may stay as long as you like." Pulling from the embrace she studied Brook, then added, "Are you hungry, dear? You're so thin!"

Brook had meant to politely refuse the offer of food, but before she could answer, Flora Grant had taken charge. "But of course you are. I have a hearty supper ready." She gazed beyond Brook. "Dusty! My dear! How are you? I've made corn bread—your favorite."

As they walked up the path to the porch, Brook smiled at the candles in each window, which winked a warm welcome. The travelers followed Mrs. Grant into the small, clean home. Snuffing out the candles, Mrs. Grant rambled on about how glad she was to have company and have her son home after such a long time. Flora Grant fairly glowed with delight at having them as guests.

She led all three from the living room, through a small

dining area, into a large kitchen, where a fireplace roared and succulent smells attacked Brook's senses.

"Everything is ready," she beamed. Jeremy Grant seated them at the table in the adjoining dining room while Flora piled food such as Brook had never seen before on plates painted with flowers and ribbons.

Brook loaded her fork with a bit of everything and had it halfway to her mouth when Captain Grant's voice and piercing eyes on her made her freeze. "Let us pray," he said, frowning at her.

She scolded herself as she bowed her head. She'd only been away from the Tatums a week, and already she'd forgotten the before-meal prayer.

"Dear heavenly Father," Jeremy Grant began, "we thank You for this food and our good friends with whom we share it. We ask Your blessing upon our meal and our friends. Bless our home and all within, and thank You for our safe journey. In Jesus' name we ask this, amen."

"Amen," the others chorused.

Before picking up her fork again, Brook mentally rehearsed every social grace Mrs. Tatum had drilled into her. She almost chuckled as she recalled her first meal with the Tatums. Indians did not eat quite the same way as white men. Anxious to be as much a member of the white race as she could, she had learned quickly and well. She breathed a silent thank-you to Mrs. Tatum and gracefully brought her fork to her mouth. Chewing slowly, with closed lips and her left hand upon her lap, she knew she'd passed the test when Jeremy Grant winked and smiled his approval.

4

A sandpapery, wet touch on her cheek made Brook's eyes fly open. Smoky! She cuddled him to her and kissed his head, rubbing gently behind his ears. "Hi, fellow. Where did you come from?"

The small, gray kitten rubbed his head against her chin and purred so loudly it kept Brook from falling back to sleep. "You sure are noisy. Do you want me awake? Okay, I'll get up."

Brook stretched and slid her legs over the side of the bed. The kitten slithered beneath the sheets, amusing himself trying to find his way out. Brook played with him momentarily then decided to search for clothes.

Opening the closet door, she stepped inside. Several dresses such as she'd never seen before hung neatly, as if waiting for her. She wasn't sure which was appropriate to wear. As she stood stroking the material of each, someone knocked lightly on her bedroom door.

Brook peeked around the corner of the closet door. Mrs.

Grant entered, smiling broadly. "Good morning, Brook. Did you sleep well, my dear?"

When Brook assured her that she had, Mrs. Grant laughed at the moving lump beneath Brook's sheet. "So your critter found you, did he?"

"Yes, thank you. I'm so fond of him."

"He's as welcome here as you are," the woman replied. "I never had a daughter, so excuse me if I fuss over you."

Brook simply smiled politely, not sure how to respond to her kindness.

Mrs. Grant beamed once again. "You found your clothes. Good. What will you wear today?"

"I'm not sure," Brook replied shyly. "Does it matter?"

"No, they're all day dresses. Take your pick. The blue would look lovely; it's the same shade as your eyes."

Brook took the blue dress and held it up. Then she looked at Mrs. Grant in puzzlement.

"What is it, dear?" Mrs. Grant asked.

"I've never worn anything like this. How do you put it on?"

"Here, let me help you."

As Mrs. Grant dressed her, Brook explained. "When I stayed with the Tatums, they let me wear my buckskin dresses. I've never seen anything such as this in my life."

"Wait until you see how lovely you will look. It's a mite big. I may have to take a few tucks. . . . Let me get my sewing basket."

While Mrs. Grant went for her sewing basket, Brook studied herself in the large mirror above the dresser. *Is this me?* she asked the image in the mirror. *I'm not an Indian. I'm a pleasing-to-look-at white lady!*

During the next few days Mrs. Grant helped Brook look and act the perfect lady. Brook liked Mrs. Grant immensely. Never had she felt so comfortable with anyone, except for Dusty, whom she saw every day, for he stayed with the Grants also. Jeremy Grant had made himself scarce the first few days, but now appeared more often. He seemed amused by the strong friendship that developed between the women, yet it was evident that something deeply troubled the captain. Brook yearned to learn what caused the haunted look to cross his face so often.

While she and Mrs. Grant made molasses cookies one afternoon, Mrs. Grant gave Brook the perfect opportunity to find her answers. Kneading the dough with strong, sure hands, Mrs. Grant asked, "You don't like my son, do you, dear?"

"He's all right, I guess," Brook answered.

"Has he done something to make you feel upset with him?"

Brook welcomed the opportunity to tell her new friend what bothered her. "Yes. As a matter of fact he has."

"Whatever has he done?" Concern filled Flora's eyes.

"His attitude is rude. He acts as if bringing me here and finding my family is too much trouble for him. He said something about now being a bad time."

"Oh, dear" was all Flora Grant said, her ever-present smile erased.

Brook continued, "I don't know what he meant by that, but he must only think of himself. Otherwise why would he be so heartless? Does he think I enjoy this? After all *I* never asked for his help!"

Mrs. Grant cut in, "Don't judge Jeremy too harshly, my dear. He's always been warm, kind, and considerate. You must overlook his faults for now. Recently something hurtful happened to him, and he is quite distressed."

Noting that Flora Grant's frustration stemmed from Brook's distrust of Jeremy Grant, Brook used this to gain more information. "He has been truly rude, selfish, and inconsiderate. Why should helping me upset him so badly? What sort of gentleman is upset by having to help a lady in distress? And why is *now* such a bad time? Should I have waited another eighteen years?"

Mrs. Grant wielded her rolling pin as if her efforts with it would burn up her anxieties; fiercely, she crushed the molasses cookie dough between the pin and the board. Then she sighed and eased up on her attack.

"Brook, I'm going to confide in you because you are like a daughter to me. Jeremy is suffering because . . . because. . . ." She pulled a handkerchief from her apron pocket and dabbed her eyes. "Jeremy was jilted."

"Jilted?" Brook repeated. Pictures of horrid illness or accident ran through the girl's mind. "What is *jilted?"*

Mrs. Grant slid her girth into a chair and took Brook's hand in hers. "My son was engaged to a girl named Melita Coopersmith. They were supposed to marry this summer. Just two months ago she broke the engagement to be free to marry someone else."

Brook thought about this for several moments before blurting, "Isn't it a good thing he found out now that her affection was not true?"

The thought seemed to take Flora Grant by surprise. Her amazed look soon turned into a knowing smile. "You're right, Brook. I'm glad it happened, too. In fact, I prayed daily for his happiness. Perhaps her jilting him was an answer to prayer. You're smarter than I thought." She leaned over and kissed Brook on the cheek. "You are very special."

Brook felt momentarily choked up. No one had ever shown her love and compassion. When she had control of her emotions, she braved another question: "How long will it take Jeremy to get over this girl and stop being sad and irritable?"

Mrs. Grant smiled. "I wish I knew, but this business with finding your family has brought things to the front."

"What do you mean?"

"Well, the fellow Melita claims to love is Angus McCallister's son, Ram. Your coming means Jeremy has to call on them, and this sort of rubs salt in his wounds. He's very proud."

Having never been in love, Brook felt little sympathy for Jeremy Grant. But she did feel sorry for Mrs. Grant, who seemed to suffer more than her son. Through Mrs. Grant, Brook could see a love she'd never thought possible. Would her real parents love her the way Mrs. Grant loved her son? Even the small tokens of love Mrs. Grant showed her warmed Brook's heart.

Yes, Brook thought, she'd like someone to love her. Was she capable of loving someone, too? She loved Smoky, so she must have the ability to love. When she found her parents, she would love them, and perhaps someday she'd meet someone special.

After Brook had been with the Grants a week, Jeremy approached her at breakfast, regarding her future. "Well, Brook, when and where do you want to start?" He poured them both a second cup of coffee.

Mrs. Grant waddled about the kitchen, clearing empty dishes and replacing them with filled ones. Brook thought if she ate much more of the delicious food, she'd have to remove the tucks in her new dresses.

"What do you mean?" she asked. "What choices do I have?"

"Are you ready to call on the McCallisters and Garrisons? Which would you like to call on first?"

Remembering his difficulty regarding the McCallisters,

she answered. "Let's begin today. I think I'd like to call on the Garrisons first."

Jeremy studied her momentarily before giving her a look of approval. "Very good. We'll leave shortly. I'm not sure how we will handle this matter, but I'm sure we'll think of something."

Brook sighed. "How will I know which family is mine?"

Jeremy shrugged. "I have a strange feeling—I have since the day you spouted off at me. Remember when I asked you to appreciate all my mother was doing for you? Before you went stomping off, you looked so like—" he stopped short.

"So like whom?" she asked. "And why did I look like someone *just then?*"

He chuckled. "Your hair is usually auburn, and when you're angry it appears to turn bright red. It's probably just the way the light happened to hit it, but—"

"One of the families in question has a redhead?" she almost demanded.

"Many families have redheads. I'm sure it means nothing. I won't plant any ideas in your head. You need an unbiased attitude to judge these families fairly. You'll feel it. You'll know which family is yours. Don't worry."

"Can Dusty go with us?" she asked.

Jeremy frowned. "Dusty is visiting his family and will be gone a few days." He raised one shaggy eyebrow. "He didn't tell you?"

She tried to hide her disappointment. "He did say something about it. I'd forgotten."

The Garrisons lived a mere mile from the Grants, in a large, two-story home with pillars that impressed Brook more than the richness. Jeremy explained that Elmer Garrison owned the large, prosperous general store.

A lovely Mexican girl answered the door and led them to a sitting room to await the Garrisons.

Brook's first impression of Elmer and Martha Garrison was disappointing. She didn't know why she felt let down; perhaps she'd expected to see a glamorous couple exactly resembling herself.

Elmer was short, wiry, and nearly bald, with black hair only adorning the sides of his large, shiny head. He seemed nervous and businesslike, hardly the type she'd expect to be capable of giving the type of love Mrs. Grant had to give her offspring.

Martha wrung her handkerchief nervously the whole time. A thin, serious woman, the deeply embedded frown lines showed she was a worrier. Her medium-brown hair, pulled tightly back into a bun, gave her a severe look.

The couple greeted them stiffly, and Brook could see they were quite curious as to why Jeremy Grant and a strange woman would call on them. She wondered how Captain Grant would handle the situation.

Grant had introduced her merely as his friend, Brook. When they were all seated and comfortable, the Garrisons looked blankly at Jeremy Grant. He cleared his throat and laughed nervously. "I suppose you wonder why we are here. Well, let me explain," he said, smiling at Brook. "My friend is visiting us and wanted to meet someone who'd lost family to Indians."

Martha gasped slightly and her hand flew to her mouth in dismay.

"You see," Grant continued, "she lost her family also and, well. . . . I thought if she talked to others who had experienced similar circumstances, it would make it easier for her. Will you help her?"

"Indians killed her family, too?" Mr. Garrison asked.

"A Comanche raid separated her from her family," Jeremy said.

"Comanche? It was Comanche who took our baby girl, too! Right, Elmer?" Martha's eyes bulged with excitement.

Elmer merely nodded.

"How old was she?" Grant asked.

"Young," Martha said. "She was only six months old."

"Do you think she's still alive and living with the Indians?" Jeremy Grant asked casually.

"We try not to think about it," Elmer curtly replied.

Jeremy Grant was not put off. "But let's just say she *did* survive and stood on your doorstep one morning. Would you know her?"

The couple seemed thoughtful.

"I would think she'd resemble someone on either side of our family. Yes, I would know her," Elmer said with conviction.

Jeremy looked at Mrs. Garrison. "Would you know your daughter?"

"Well," Martha began, "I'm not sure. Her hair was dark, her eyes brown, and," she perked with sudden excitement, "I remember she had a birthmark on her right leg. So, yes, I would know her."

Jeremy Grant flung a quick look at Brook. She shook her head slightly.

They stayed and made small talk before saying good-bye. The couple expressed sympathy for Brook and her family, and Brook assured them that sharing their tragedy with her helped cope with her loss.

Brook left the Garrisons' home elated. Jeremy Grant, however, seemed disappointed.

As they rode side by side toward home, Brook expressed her relief that Elmer and Martha were not her parents. She chattered on and on about it before noticing Jeremy's silence. "Is something wrong?" she asked.

"When do you want to visit the McCallisters?" he countered.

"We may as well get it over with."

He hesitated, then agreed. "Tomorrow we visit Angus McCallister."

5

Brook opened her eyes to bright spring sunshine. Smoky, basking in the strong Texas rays, stretched lazily at the bottom of the bed, repositioning himself to make the most of the sun's warmth. Brook stretched also.

Today she would visit the McCallisters. Jeremy had said Angus's wife was the second Mrs. McCallister. If Angus was her father, that meant her mother was dead. A strong sense of disappointment swept over her. She wanted a mother so badly, especially after meeting Jeremy's loving mother. Jeremy had also said that the son was probably a stepson; therefore she'd have no sisters or brothers. Again a wave of disappointment engulfed her. Perhaps, she thought, searching for a bright spot, the McCallisters were not her family either. Maybe a loving older couple would turn out to be her own parents. She banished the thought. No sense setting herself up for disappointment.

A soft knock on her door broke off her daydreams. "Come in," she called, pulling her sheet up to her chin.

"It's only me," Flora Grant whispered as she entered.

Brook smiled. "Good morning."

Mrs. Grant eased into the chair beside her bed. "Just came to tell you breakfast is ready and. . . ." She paused for breath. Poor Mrs. Grant was so corpulant that often she had to catch her breath after a minor exertion such as climbing the stairs.

"And," she continued, "to invite you to our worship service. We usually visit the local church, but we can't today because we must keep you a secret until we find your family. When we can't go to church, we make our own. Will you join us?"

Brook hesitated, remembering the Tatums' elaborate, long services. Considering her place as a guest in this lovely home, she answered as her conscience commanded. "Yes, of course I'll join you."

"Wonderful. Jeremy will be pleased," Flora answered, pulling herself to her feet once more. "Services begin in an hour. You'd best get dressed and breakfasted." She patted the kitten. "Such a good fellow you are, Smoky."

"Is Dusty back yet?" Brook asked.

"No, he won't be back for a few days. His family lives on a reservation in Oklahoma quite a ride away."

Brook swung her legs from the bed. "I'll be down in a few minutes."

Mrs. Grant left with a sad, thoughtful look that Brook thought she understood. *She's disappointed because I seem more interested in friendship with Dusty than her son.*

After a hearty breakfast, Brook was escorted to the living room, where Flora played a hymn on the piano that stood against one wall. Grant smiled the first real welcome ever as she apprehensively edged into a chair.

As soon as Mrs. Grant's song ended, her son cleared his

throat. He stood before the fireplace with a large book balanced in one hand.

"Our message this morning," he announced, "is from my favorite book, James. We'll look at chapter five, verses thirteen through eighteen, on prayer.

" 'Is any among you afflicted? let him pray. Is any merry? let him sing psalms . . . ,' " he began to read.

Brook listened carefully, anticipating a long, boring recitation.

" '. . . And he prayed again, and the heaven gave rain, and the earth brought forth her fruit.' " Jeremy closed the book softly. Mrs. Grant sat beside her, with hands folded serenely in her lap.

Jeremy stood before them and talked, not preached, to them. "There is power in prayer," he said. "But you may not receive unless you ask. God is your Father. He loves you. You are His child, and He wants to give you what is best for you. It is very important that you talk to Him. Just as earthly parents and children must communicate, so must you converse with your Father in heaven."

Brook found herself paying careful attention. This was different from Mr. Tatum's dull sermons. Jeremy was not preaching or reading words she didn't understand directly from the book. He was talking to her in plain language. She cocked her auburn head, as if to ask, "How do I talk to God?"

As if in direct answer, Jeremy's next statement was clear. "Talk to God just as you would your earthly father. You don't need words from a book or fancy prayers. Just tell Him how you feel. Yes, He does know everything already. Sometimes parents know what their children will say, yet they still long to hear those thoughts spoken. As parents must communicate with children, so must we communicate with God, our Father. God wants you to take the time to talk to Him. It shows you care enough to share your thoughts, hopes, and wishes with Him. He thrives on it."

While Jeremy went on to describe the different ways God answers prayer, Brook's mind still dwelt on talking to God as one would a real father. She didn't know how to talk to a real father either, so how should she talk to God?

If God was her Father, she reasoned, then no matter what happened, she had family. God was family. Hadn't Jeremy said so? He'd also said God loved her. Therefore, no matter what happened with the Garrisons or the McCallisters, she would not worry. She had a Father, a loving, understanding Father who'd love her the way Mrs. Grant loved Jeremy.

The McCallisters lived about two miles from the town, in a sprawling ranch house with many surrounding buildings. Brook and Jeremy stood on the large veranda, waiting for an answer to his knock. Nervously Brook played with the parasol Mrs. Grant had given her to protect her skin from the sun. She liked it better than the floppy hat she'd always worn while she'd stayed with the Indians, because, unlike the squaws, she sunburned easily. Brook tilted her head to get the most of a breeze, for the day grew hot. The ruffles of her gray and red dress bounced lightly in the wind. She patted them back into place and twisted her red parasol again.

Finally, an old woman dressed in black opened the door and peeked out. Bright blue eyes were all that was left to show she'd once been attractive. Opening the door just a crack, she squinted up as Jeremy spoke, watching his face carefully.

When he asked if Mr. or Mrs. McCallister was at home and could see them, she nodded. Then the cautious old woman switched her glance to Brook, who instantly smiled to show they were harmless and friendly. Instead of assurance, a look of pure horror spread across the woman's face, and she shrieked, holding one hand to her breast.

"Goodness, what's wrong, Jeremy?" Brook gasped.

Catching her as she fell, he murmured, "I don't know. What happened?"

Holding the woman in his arms, he called out, "Anyone home? Mrs. McCallister? Angus? Anyone here?"

A short, stocky woman came to help Jeremy. "What happened to her? Who are you?" she asked as she eased Jeremy's burden into an upholstered chair near the front door. Jeremy and Brook followed her into the living room.

Brook looked about curiously. She loved the room, which looked and smelled like nature. Her eyes scanned the wooden walls and the stone fireplace with live plants growing upon the sturdy wooden mantel.

Jeremy introduced himself and Brook and explained that he'd hardly told the old woman their business when she had screamed and collapsed.

"She'll be fine," the woman said without affection. "The old prune is tougher than all of us." As the old woman drooped in the chair, the younger one introduced herself: "I'm Angus's wife, Ada, and this," she nodded toward the other woman, "is his mother, Maggie. Please have a seat." When her guests dropped together onto the large sofa with thick oak legs and arms, she chose the matching armchair across from them. She did not relax, but perched on the edge of her seat as if ready to leave on an impulse.

"What can I do for you?" she questioned politely.

"Is Angus at home?" Jeremy asked.

"Yes, but he's indisposed at the moment."

Glancing uneasily at poor Maggie, he expressed concern. "Are you certain she's all right?"

"Quite. She's merely fainted."

"I see." Jeremy looked about the room nervously, as if

thinking his way out of a dilemma. "We did want to see Angus . . . as well as yourself, that is."

"May I ask why?"

From her chair near the door, Maggie began to come back to reality. Jeremy explained, "It's about his daughter."

Brook gave him a surprised look, then glanced at Maggie, who had gasped more loudly than Ada McCallister. Maggie McCallister stared, wide-eyed at Brook.

"Daughter?" Ada repeated, as if she'd never heard the word before.

Maggie pounded the arms of her chair with both hands and made a cackling noise that Brook could only identify as a laugh because of the sparkle in the old woman's eyes.

"Pay her no mind," ordered Ada. "She's—" Instead of using words, Ada pointed to her own temple, made a wry face, and whispered, "You know what I mean?"

When Brook and Jeremy nodded, Ada regained her composure. "Yes. Angus had a daughter, but she and his first wife were killed by Comanche many years ago. Of course I never met either, so I cannot tell you much about them, except what I've heard. What would you like to know?"

Jeremy watched Maggie carefully as he spoke to Ada. "What about Maggie? Surely she remembers. May we ask her?"

Maggie watched them all with a knowing look and bright, sparkling eyes.

"She probably could tell you plenty, except she doesn't speak. She took sick several years ago and hasn't said a word since then."

Jeremy's face showed disappointment. "Well, then, we must see Angus. Please take us to him."

"He doesn't see anyone. He's ill."

Brook watched Maggie carefully. The woman might not speak with her mouth, but her face spoke volumes. Maggie didn't like Ada or at least didn't like what she had said.

Jeremy grew agitated. "We *must* see him. We'll make an appointment."

Ada stood and spoke softly but harshly. "That is not possible. I'll show you to the door."

The old woman slapped the arms of her chair again, then stamped her feet loudly, as if to gain attention.

"See what I mean?" Ada said.

"Perhaps," Brook spoke for the first time, "she wants to tell us something."

Maggie's face took on an excited look, but it drooped suddenly as Ada opened the front door.

"Sorry I couldn't help you. Good day."

Jeremy shrugged, then reluctantly followed her to the door.

Maggie's pleading eyes held Brook's, and Brook stood stubbornly, with arms folded before her. "I'm not leaving."

"Brook!" Jeremy looked back at her in amazement. "But you must. . . ." He glanced from Brook to Ada. "We've been shown the door."

"This home also belongs to Angus *and* Maggie, and she'd like me to stay until I see Angus. Isn't that right, Maggie?"

The old woman nodded excitedly and began pounding the chair arms again.

"Please, miss," Ada implored. "Don't start trouble. The old lady is nutty enough now. Don't encourage her." She held the door wider. "Please leave. Quickly."

Jeremy Grant looked from one woman to the other in confusion before letting his eyes rest on Brook. He didn't scowl, as she'd expected, but smiled proudly. "My friend has a point, Mrs. McCallister. We *are* Maggie's guests."

Ada let the door slam shut. "But the woman is crazy!"

"I think she is merely frustrated by not being able to talk," Brook said, smiling at the old woman affectionately. Maggie smiled in return and nodded excitedly. "I believe Maggie will take us to Angus."

Nodding, the old woman stood and took Brook's hand.

"Now see here," cried Ada. "I'll get my son! Ram will put an end to this foolishness."

But Brook's next remark knocked the friskiness from Ada McCallister and made her mouth drop in shock. "Maggie is taking me to see the man who may be my father."

Already leading them down the long hall, Maggie turned to see the shocked expression on Ada's face and cackled loudly.

Brook and Jeremy allowed Maggie to pull them down the narrow passage and around a corner, until they stood before a large wooden door. Maggie held up her hand, motioning them to halt as she squeezed through the portal and closed it behind her. Evidently she wanted to prepare Angus for the visit.

Jeremy stood close, for the hall was extremely narrow. He gently put his hands upon Brook's shoulders. "Now don't get your hopes up," he whispered.

"What do you mean?"

"He may not be your father, or he may not be what you'd like your father to be."

She looked up at him in puzzlement. "Do you know something I don't?"

"I haven't seen the man in years, but . . . ," he let his voice drop. "I just don't want to see you disappointed."

She smiled. "No one can choose parents."

"Yes, but Ada said he was ill. He may be sicker than you think, or—"

Before he could finish, the door opened, and Maggie appeared. Taking one hand of each, she gently pulled them into the darkened room.

6

On the way back to Captain Grant's home, Brook remained silent. Jeremy rode beside her, quiet also. What thoughts labored in that handsome, proud head? Brook could only wonder, for he said so little. Yet she felt herself beginning to like him, despite her first impression. Perhaps Mrs. Grant had pleaded his case well, or maybe his recent considerate conduct had changed her mind. Whatever the reason, her feelings toward him had definitely begun to alter. Yet she dearly missed Dusty.

Her fondness for Mrs. Grant, Jeremy, and Dusty comforted her somewhat in her disappointment today. What more family did she need? She had God, too, she reminded herself. A true Father. Her earthly one had proved to be less than what she had longed for.

As they neared the populated area of Fort Worth and began taking Jeremy's shortcuts—winding up and down one street after another—Brook replayed the afternoon in her mind.

The old woman—Brook liked her. Was that woman her grandmother? Despite her inability to speak, Brook felt no disappointment about Maggie. She was intriguing and spunky, and Brook liked to think she had inherited those qualities from her—if indeed they were related.

Ada was a difficult woman to like, yet hadn't Mr. and Mrs. Tatum preached to her so often that she should love her fellowman? She would try harder to like Ada, so she could be in God's good favor. She truly wanted to please her heavenly Father.

Tears threatened to spill at the thought of her first look at Angus McCallister—her father? She shivered. The room had been dark, despite Maggie's attempts to let in the sunlight by opening the heavy drapes. The man called Angus had lain upon his bed, reeking of firewater. The very thought sent chills down her spine. Hadn't Big Bear smelled the same? Recalling the beatings she'd received only when he'd smelled like firewater sent fear through her whole body. Was her father another Big Bear? Would she be denied a loving family her whole life?

So deep in thought was Brook that Jeremy had to tap her riding boot to gain her attention. She had been unaware they had reached the Grant home. Jeremy was already off his horse and waiting to help her off the mare.

"I'm sorry, I was daydreaming," she apologized.

He grasped her waist instead of her hands this time, giving Brook a strange, warm, secure feeling. Once on the ground she looked up into his eyes, only to find there a look she'd never seen on anyone before, a forlorn, protective look. Or could it be sympathy? She prayed not.

"I'm sorry about Angus," he said, hands still grasping her waist. "I'd heard some town gossip that he'd been drinking too much, but never trust hearsay."

"I'm sorry, too," she replied.

"I'll do everything I can to help you," he said.

She pulled away from his lingering hands. "What can be done? The man is a drunk. Do you think he's my father?"

"Yes, I do."

"What makes you think so?"

"His looks, Maggie's—note his red hair, her bright-blue eyes and high cheekbones—and a gut feeling."

"All right," she said, swallowing her disappointment and straightening her backbone, in an effort to accept reality. "What is our next move?"

He led her toward the house. "That's what I've been meditating on. I'm thinking another visit, but this time earlier in the day—before he can get too bagged. Perhaps," he said thoughtfully, "through our helper, Maggie."

"What do you mean?" she asked.

"We must find a way to let Maggie—and Maggie alone—know we are coming to see Angus. I think she is anxious to help and can assist us on that end. Maybe she can even keep him sober."

"We'll send her a letter!" Brook exclaimed, eyes bright.

Jeremy smiled and cuffed her chin lightly. "But what if Ada intercepts it?"

Brook cocked her head in puzzlement. "I don't mean to act dumb, but I'm still learning. What is *intercept?*"

"My fault; I'm sorry. You seem so adept at English I forget you only recently learned it. *Intercept* means 'to stop something short of its purpose or goal.' Should Ada receive the letter instead of Maggie, she may stop it from reaching Maggie. She didn't want us seeing him, perhaps because of his condition—or some other reason."

"I see," she said thoughtfully. "We could have someone deliver it to Maggie personally."

"Yes, but who? Someone who never visits Maggie might

arouse too much suspicion and tip off Ada." He scratched his head and opened the back door for her.

As usual delicious smells met her as soon as she entered the warm, homey kitchen. A large pot was boiling above a roaring flame, and its top rattled from the outpour of aromatic steam. A freshly iced chocolate cake sat on the wooden table, and Reva, Flora's hired girl, mashed potatoes at the counter. Flora smiled a warm greeting as she gingerly removed freshly baked bread from her large oven.

"Hope you two are hungry. Sauerbraten with gingersnap gravy—Grandma Bauer's favorite—is our menu," Flora announced.

"You might be able to force some on me." Jeremy winked.

"It smells heavenly," responded Brook.

"And I have one other surprise for dinner," she said, waving her hand toward the open dining-room door.

A dark, clean-shaven man, in a suit complete with string tie stood in a gentlemanly fashion beside the tall china cabinet.

"Dusty!" exclaimed Brook, running to greet him. "It's so wonderful to see you. I've so much to tell you!"

Dusty smiled boyishly.

Jeremy merely nodded in his direction and muttered some polite words of greeting with no feeling behind them. To everyone he said clearly, "Allow me to wash the dust off, and I'll join you promptly." He bowed and disappeared.

His rudeness to Dusty shocked Flora more than it did Brook. She closed her gaping mouth and shook her head, "Just can't figure my son out these days." To Dusty, she apologized, adding, "You know what stress he's been under. . . ."

Looking at both women, the Indian nodded, "I understand Captain Grant perfectly. Pay it no mind."

Brook also excused herself to wash, and her mind did not dwell on Jeremy's rudeness to his best friend, but on the drunken Angus McCallister and his mother, Maggie.

After dinner, in the living room, Brook conveyed her news to Dusty while Flora and Jeremy listened and added to the conversation as needed—Flora, excitedly; Jeremy, sullenly. When Brook got to the end of the story, she described Angus's drunken state and explained how they planned to get a message to his mother.

"Now," added Flora with a sly smile, "I can be of help. Few people around here call on the McCallisters, for they keep to themselves, but there is one caller for Maggie who might help us."

All eyes flew to Flora Grant.

"Dr. Quade goes out to see Maggie periodically; we can ask him to give her a message."

Brook looked at Jeremy. He seemed to be digesting the idea.

"Isn't Quade a family friend, too?" he asked his mother.

"I suppose, but he's treated Maggie since her illness. I would think a family doctor could be trusted."

"Fine," stated Jeremy, "the doctor it shall be."

"That's settled," said Flora. She looked at Dusty, "How is your family?"

Dusty's smile faded. "Not as well as I'd hoped. The reservation is not what the government vowed." He looked at Jeremy Grant evenly. "Few of the promises made by you and your fellow officers at Fort Sill were kept."

Jeremy sat straight and asked indignantly, "What do you mean? What promises?"

"Many of the Indians are ill, and no one cares. Your government promised medicines and doctors. They ordered my people to cut their hair, dress as white men, and to get rid of tepees and live in huts. They insist Indians suddenly change the life-style they've had since birth. They made our warriors do garden work, like squaws, and took all the fire from their hearts. Now my people are pitiful. They cough from sleeping inside a shanty with no ventilation and fumes from inside heat. Our strong warriors have become weak and puny.

"The government promised to supply meat, and we never get it on time, and my people are starving. The last shipment of food was so late it was rotted. . . ." Dusty glanced at his bewildered audience, "Do you want me to continue?"

"I had no idea," Jeremy said. "I only relayed to you what Colonel Grierson was told from Washington."

"Washington, bah!" Dusty spat. "My people are sick and dying!"

"Are there Comanche there, too, sick and dying?" Brook ventured.

"Yes." Dusty said. "Mostly all just over the Red River are Kiowa and Comanche—further north are several other tribes."

Brook thought about her best friend, Singing Bird, and her cousin Little Fox, and her heart flooded with concern. "Captain Grant, what can we do?"

Jeremy frowned. "I can do nothing here in Fort Worth. It will have to wait until this matter with you and your family is settled. Then I will return to Fort Sill and confront the colonel with these facts—actually *you* will, Dusty. I'll make sure you get a meeting with him. You can give a detailed, first-hand account of the conditions on the reservation."

Dusty nodded and smiled at his friend. "That, my friend, is fair enough." He settled his smile on Brook. "Well, I guess our first business is your family. Since I am indirectly involved here, may I add something?"

"Of course!" Flora, Jeremy, and Brook chorused.

"May I try some Indian tactics?"

"Indian tactics?" Flora asked.

Brook nodded knowingly.

"Just a little sneaking around the McCallister place and spying a mite," he offered.

"It can't hurt," said Jeremy. "But we'll progress with our letter and, I hope, another visit, while you play Indian games."

"One thing," Dusty added urgently. "I'm not so sure the doctor can be trusted. I see him in town with that Ram, Ada's son—and we know *he* can't be trusted."

Jeremy frowned. "We have no choice."

"I could deliver the letter," Dusty offered.

"But how?" Flora asked. "Surely Ada would find out."

"Trust me. Just describe the person the letter is meant for, and it will be in her hands—without anyone knowing. I'm a scout, remember?"

Flora gave Jeremy a sheet of thin stationery and an inked pen. He wrote:

> Dear Maggie:
>
> We will return to see Angus McCallister on Wednesday morning and trust you will prepare him for our visit. It is urgent that we settle this matter as soon as possible. Please answer the door—alone—when we knock. It may not be a good idea to tell anyone other than Angus of our plans. Thank you for your help.
>
> Our messenger is a friend, Dusty, and you may trust him completely.
>
> Sincerely,
> Captain Grant
> and "Brook"

After everyone had read the missive and agreed on its contents, Jeremy folded it and handed it to Dusty. "Go to it, my friend."

Taking the letter and putting it in his breast pocket, Dusty said, "I'll need a good night's sleep to be at my best tomorrow." He waved good-night and disappeared up the stairs.

Flora squeezed out of her chair, "Guess I'll make a night of it, too." She kissed Brook, "Good night, dear." Jeremy bent for her to embrace him. "Good night, Son. Snuff out the window candles before you go to bed."

When Flora's creaking steps could no longer be heard going up the wooden stairs, Brook, too, excused herself for the night.

"Wait." Jeremy halted her steps. "It's a beautiful evening, and not so late. Would you like to take a short walk?"

Relishing the thought of the fresh night air, she agreed. She missed sleeping outdoors and could relate to the Indians' sufferings on the reservation. She thought how many times she had crawled out Tatum's window and slept atop the eaves until the first rays of dawn warned her to return before she was discovered.

They walked the quiet streets, talking only when they saw something to point out. The air must have been close to body temperature, for Brook could feel no difference in the temperature, no chill or heat. The air was perfect, without a breeze or cloud.

After walking about a mile, they headed back toward home. As they neared the house, Grant seemed to slow his pace, and Brook felt him slightly squeeze her hand, tucked under his arm. He seemed about to say something when he tensed at the sound of a horse galloping toward them. Gunshots broke into the stillness of the night.

"What—?" Jeremy muttered, pulling her with him against the large cottonwood in front of his house. The large bole hid them from view.

The rider approached at breakneck speed, without letting

up, and he continued to shoot his pistol. When the horse and rider rode past the Grant house, they slowed only long enough for the rider to throw something at the house, smashing the front window. The culprit rode on, shooting randomly.

Looking from the rider to the house, in shock, Brook and Jeremy said in unison as they ran toward the front door, "The candle!"

7

With lightning speed, Brook and Jeremy ran for the front door. Jeremy reached it first and burst into the living room. By the time Brook caught up, hungry flames leaped from the carpet to the drape. Jeremy ripped the fiery panel from the window, threw it over the flaming spot on the floor, and began stomping on the fabric. "Get water!" he yelled.

Dashing into the kitchen, Brook grabbed the bucket, which someone had left almost full. Yet by the time she handed it to Jeremy, she was sure she'd lost half of that in her haste.

Moments later, Dusty and Flora raced into the room, Dusty dressed haphazardly and Flora wrapped in a bathrobe. Both loudly demanded explanations. Dousing the entire area with water, Jeremy told them to wait until the fire was out.

From the sofa, the three watched Jeremy snuff the life from the fire. When it appeared under control, he reached under the chair opposite the table that the candle had sat upon and drew out a large rock. Flora gasped.

Jeremy frowned at the rock, then untied a cord wound around it, opened a soiled paper, and studied it intently. His face paled.

"What is it?" Brook voiced the question in all their minds.

Jeremy shook his head and rubbed his temple with his free hand, leaving a soot mark on his brow. Folding the missive carefully, he put it into his breast pocket. Replacing the wet, wrinkled, scorched drape and pulling it shut, he turned to the awaiting questioning looks.

Jeremy recounted the walk he and Brook had taken and the frantic horseback rider. "When I didn't recognize him, I hoped he was merely an anonymous prankster—a drunken cowboy having a little fun, throwing a rock at a random home. But this note," he withdrew the folded letter from his pocket, "proves me wrong."

"What does it say?" his mother asked, eyes wide.

He gave Brook a sympathetic look. "Maybe we can discuss this later—"

"It's about Brook, isn't it?" asked Dusty. "She has a right to know," he added, also looking at her with concern.

Jeremy sighed. He reluctantly opened the paper and reread it. Shaking his head, he handed it to Dusty. "I can't." At Dusty's reproachful look, he added, "Go ahead, then, you read it."

Taking the paper, Dusty read aloud without screening it first.

> Get rid of the white squaw. We don't want no Indian trash living here. She ain't related to no one in Fort Worth. Send her back to the Comanche. If she stays, there will be more trouble.

Dusty folded the paper with a frown. "It isn't signed."

"Yet," said Jeremy, "while the grammar is a farce, the spelling and handwriting are perfect. Almost makes me think we are purposely being misled as to the intelligence of the writer. He wants us to think it was written by an illiterate cowboy."

"I must find somewhere else to stay," blurted Brook.

"That's ridiculous," said Flora.

"Unheard of," affirmed Jeremy.

"I cannot bring this type of trouble to your home," Brook stated. "I will not."

"But we don't mind one bit. Do we, Jeremy?" Flora spoke with a shaky, unsure voice.

Knowing Flora's loving nature, despite her fear or anger, Brook knew she'd always be welcome in the Grant home.

Jeremy knelt down to where Brook sat on her chair and took her small hands in his. "Brook, you're our guest. No one tells us whom we may entertain in our home. I will get to the bottom of this. *Someone will answer for this deed!*"

Confused, Brook looked from Flora to Jeremy. "But it's my fault. Look at your carpet and drapes! Why the whole house could have—"

"No!" Jeremy interjected, squeezing her hands. "It is the fault of the demented person who threw the rock or ordered it thrown." Then more gently, he added, "Someone is trying to scare you away, but it will not keep us from what we came here to do. We will find your family, and you will stay *here* until we do."

The next morning, after breakfast, Jeremy and Dusty departed. Dusty went to deliver the letter to Maggie and sneak around and see what he could find out, and Jeremy claimed he had business in town.

As Flora poured Brook another cup of coffee, she sighed. "Do you think Angus is your father?"

"Jeremy thinks so; he may be right. I'm confused right now and very disappointed in Angus McCallister."

"H-m-m-m," Flora murmured thoughtfully. "I don't blame you. Did anyone ever say what Angus's daughter's name was—or is?"

"No," said Brook. "It's strange not to know your own name."

"I would think so," Flora patted her arm. "Let me see, if I had a beautiful daughter like you I'd have named her. . . ," she studied Brook's face carefully. "A soft name, because your face and features are soft. *Mary* or *Marian*, for I prefer biblical names. Another ideal name for you would be *Angela*, because you often appear angelic and—" A knock at the kitchen door cut her off.

"Now who can that be at the back door? Excuse me, dear," she said, rising.

"I'm coming," she called as she waddled to the door.

Until this moment, Brook had never known Flora to be at a loss for words. She couldn't see the visitor, for Flora's large bulk hid it, but Flora remained silent for several long moments. "M-Melita! How . . . g-good to see you," she finally uttered. Brook had never heard Flora force cheerfulness.

"Won't you come in?"

Melita Cooper-something, thought Brook. *That's the woman who did something horrid to Jeremy: gelded, gilded, or jilted him, or something like that.* Brook couldn't wait for Flora to step aside, so she could see this Jezebel.

As Flora finally moved, Brook struggled to keep a shocked look from her face. Melita Coopersmith stood there, tall, thin, and dressed in a turquoise satin Brook longed to touch. The woman was beautiful in a way Brook had never before seen—though she hadn't seen many white women. She longed to run her hands through Melita's hair and wondered if its unusual color, which dazzled her eyes, resembled a buttercup or dandelion.

Melita's round face glowed with rosy cheeks and large blue eyes several shades deeper than Brook's. However, on closer inspection, Brook noticed Melita's beauty had a touch of cosmetic help. Clever darkening around her eyes gave them a larger, wider look.

Despite her pleasing looks and delightful smile, Brook took an instant dislike to Melita. Wasn't this the woman who had hurt Captain Grant so badly that he had been reluctant to help find her family? Yes, Brook decided, she would not like this Melita Coopersmith.

"Won't you join us for coffee?" Flora offered a bit stiffly. "I'd like you to meet our houseguest, Brook. Brook, this is a family friend, Melita Coopersmith."

Melita smiled briefly at Brook but looked after Flora with concern. "Flora, it isn't like you to hold a grudge."

"What makes you say that?" Flora asked, red faced.

"You wear your heart on your sleeve."

"I never *could* hide my feelings," Flora admitted. "Sit down, Melita. I'll get you a cup."

Melita sat and removed her gloves. She smiled at Brook again. While Flora poured her coffee, Melita said sweetly, "It's nice to meet you, Brook. Will you be here long?"

Before Brook could answer, Flora said, "She'll be here for good, we hope. She's planning to stay in Fort Worth. Jeremy brought her back from Oklahoma."

Brook knew, despite Flora's loving nature, this rose had thorns. His mother had purposely misled Melita into thinking that she and Jeremy were friendlier than they were. Brook would have to remember that anyone who messed with Jeremy would answer to Flora.

"Perhaps, I should go upstairs. You two probably have a lot to talk about." Brook excused herself and stood.

"No," Flora cried, with a definite edge to her voice. "Sit down and drink your coffee." With one eye on Melita, she added, "Melita may be able to give you some information on the McCallisters. She is practically related to them."

Slightly amused, Brook obeyed, sipping her coffee with wide-eyed anticipation.

"Flora!" exclaimed Melita. "Will you allow me to explain why I did what I did?"

"It wasn't so much *what* you did, but *the way* you did it," remonstrated Flora.

"I agree with you," the girl answered humbly. Melita patted Flora's hand. "I'm sorry for the whole thing. I came to apologize to you and Jeremy. Is he home?"

"No, Jeremy is in town." Flora rubbed her temples and took a deep breath. "Heavenly Father, help me," she whispered. "What is wrong with me?" Returning Melita's hand, she gave it a quick pat. "I apologize, too. I've told myself and the Lord so many times that I'd forgiven you, yet when you showed up here—I don't know what came over me. Will you forgive me, Melita?"

The blond woman nodded. "I understand. You love your son more than anything. But people make mistakes, and I admit that I acted impulsively. Jeremy was away; Ram was here. Ram seemed so exciting—"

"And now?" Flora asked suspiciously.

"Now?" Melita repeated, toying with her cup. "Now, I don't know. But I wanted to apologize to you both."

"Apology accepted," Flora said, "but while the wound is healing, it's still sore."

"What does that mean?" Melita asked.

"I'm not even sure myself, except it may take a while for me to forget and trust you completely. I'm even afraid to ask if you're going to try and get back with Jeremy. Are you?"

"To be honest with you, I don't know. I'm still seeing Ram, but I doubt it will ever amount to anything. I'm fond of him, truly, but there's something untamed about him that frightens me." She shivered. "I didn't come here to win Jeremy back, if that's what you mean. I felt I owed you both an apology, that's all."

Flora rose and hugged the girl. "Just tread lightly for a while, all right."

"Of course," Melita said, returning the embrace. "Now what's this about your friend? How did you come to be a visitor in the Grant home?" She swung to face Brook. "Are you Flora's guest or Jeremy's?"

"Brook is *my* guest," Jeremy's authoritative voice caused all three ladies to jump. He walked into the kitchen, out of the living room, from an angle none of the women faced. "I brought her home with me from Oklahoma," he added, pouring himself a cup of coffee. He stood beside Brook.

Brook studied Melita's face. Surprise and what Brook thought could have been jealousy spread across it, but only momentarily. She quickly hid her thoughts behind a large smile.

"How wonderful. And it's so delightful to see you again. How are you, Jeremy?"

"I've never been better," he replied cheerfully.

"Could I have a private word with you before I leave?" she asked. "It will only take a minute."

"It isn't necessary, Melita. Your apology is accepted. I hold no hard feelings. Actually it worked out for the best. Those things usually do." He held out his hand. "I sincerely hope we can be friends."

Melita met his grasp, and they shook hands. "I'm so glad. I felt terrible about things. As your mother said, it isn't so much what I did, but how I did it. It's a relief to know all is forgiven. Yes, we *will* be friends."

Before leaving, Melita turned to Brook. "We didn't get a chance to talk, but whatever your connection is with the McCallisters, I'll be glad to help wherever I can. Just let me know. I live behind the bakery. Flora will direct you. It was a pleasure meeting you."

Brook thanked her but felt angry inside. How could she dislike such a remarkable young woman? Despite everything, Brook didn't dislike Melita Coopersmith, she liked her, liked her very much.

Approaching the McCallister's ranch, mid-morning on Wednesday, Brook purposefully studied its perimeters more carefully than before. After all, this might soon be her home. Off to one side were several fenced areas. One contained horses; the others appeared empty. The house sat between the fenced areas and a narrow stream framed by sandy hills and sparse evergreen trees, with misty purple mountains in the distance.

The ranch house was not impressive, like the Garrisons' city home. Yet it seemed appropriate to its rustic setting. Made of logs, the house was long and appeared L shaped. A long porch ran along the front, and several old rocking chairs graced its length. The colorful chair covers gave the outside of the house its only splatter of color, besides the bright-red welcome mat.

Smoke streamed from one of the three chimneys, testifying that despite the stillness, someone was up and about inside.

Tying the horses to a hitching post, Brook and Jeremy crossed the yard and approached the front door. After one small knock, the door swung open, and Maggie stuck out her head. Smiling with both mouth and bright-blue eyes, she waved them inside.

She put one finger to her lips, to silence them, and they followed Maggie on tiptoe down the long hall to Angus McCallister's room. Again Maggie motioned them to wait while she went in ahead.

This time Jeremy put his arms around Brook and drew her close. His nearness triggered an emotion in Brook, and she prepared to back away. His soft whisper in her ear stopped her, "Promise me you won't expect too much."

"What do you mean?" she whispered back, confused by his closeness and his words.

"If Angus is a disappointment, don't let it upset you too much. You still have God. He's your Father, and you will never be disappointed in Him. You always have Mother and me. We're good as family—and will be for as long as you'd like," he whispered tenderly in her ear.

"My disappointment matters to you?" A new and unexpected warmth surged through her.

He looked deep in her eyes and swallowed. "It matters." His voice was calm, his gaze steady.

"Do you feel sympathy for me?" she asked boldly, pulling away.

He hesitated. "A little, but—"

"Don't feel sorry for me. I'm tough, I lived with Indians, remember?" She took a deep breath and tried to relax. "The last thing in the world I want from you or anyone is sympathy."

Jeremy started to reply, but Maggie appeared and motioned them into the well-lit room.

Standing inside the door, Brook gazed around the masculine apartment. The quilt-covered bed was empty, and her eyes moved beyond to the chair by the open-draped window. There sat a burly, weathered man with the brightest, reddest hair Brook had ever seen. He had large, bushy eyebrows to match, sprinkled with gray.

His eyes followed Brook into the room and never left hers. No one spoke. Maggie and Jeremy were merely bystanders to the meeting of two matching souls. At last he spoke, "Genevieve!"

8

Maggie ran to Angus's side and gently slapped his hand to get his attention, but his eyes remained fixed on Brook. "It's my own Genevieve!"

Taking the man's head and turning it to face her, Maggie made him look at her. She shook her head violently, then released his head and rocked her arms, as if she held a baby.

The red-headed man's face showed understanding. He smiled. "Not Genevieve. Yes, I know, my Genevieve is dead. Yet she could so easily be her, except for her hair. But no, it isn't Genevieve. This is our baby, my long-lost baby—Laurel!"

Maggie jumped up and down in excitement, nodding in agreement.

Brook and Jeremy's eyes met. Jeremy mouthed the name softly, "Laurel," and smiled.

Brook felt a warm glow pierce her. She ran to Angus and put her arms around his neck and hugged him. Just as Jeremy had told her, she *knew!* This was her father.

She now had a name and a family. Laurel—what a lovely name—just like the nature she loved. *Laurel McCallister*. She belonged.

As if noticing Jeremy for the first time, Angus offered him an outstretched hand. Jeremy walked to him, and they shook hands heartily.

"Thank you for returning my daughter to me. I am in your debt, sir," Angus said, with emotion in his voice and tears in his eyes.

Laurel watched Jeremy shift his eyes downward and answer softly, "My pleasure. You owe me nothing." He looked at Laurel. "I suppose you'll move in here now?"

Laurel looked anxiously at Angus.

"Of course she will!" he bellowed with a powerful voice. "She's a McCallister. This is where she belongs."

His masterful voice frightened Laurel, and she shrank back somewhat. Noticing, Angus patted her hand gently. "No need to ever fear me, lassie. I may be big, and I may roar like a lion, but I'd sooner put a lance through my own chest than harm one hair on your head."

Drawing courage from his words, Laurel straightened her back and boldly asked him what she feared asking the most: "What about the firewater? I will *not* live with you, father or not, if you continue to drink that poison."

Her question seemed to stun Angus and Maggie, but Jeremy smiled proudly at her. He seemed to admire her spunk, Laurel noted.

"Firewater?" Angus asked.

"Excuse me, sir," Jeremy said. "I believe she means whiskey. We were here last week. . . ." He looked about uncomfortably.

"That was last week!" he roared. "And this is this week!" Angus hugged Laurel to him. "I have in my arms the result of my love for Genevieve Beauforte McCallister: my own lost daughter, Laurel. What reason do I have for drinking firewater now?"

"Promise?" Laurel asked in a small, girlish voice.

Angus scratched his head. "Now, lass, I gotta be honest with you. I've been drinking that rotgut for years. With you and your mother gone, I found life easier to face that way. It won't be easy, but I promise to try."

"But you married Ada. Surely you loved her."

"Love Ada?" He laughed. "Yes, I guess you might call it that." He faltered for the right words. "It wasn't the same, Laurel. I tried. Ada's a good woman, but. . . . Your mother and I had—something—something no one else can understand."

"Ada didn't want us to see you. Why?" Laurel asked. "Because of your condition or because she doesn't want me here?"

Angus looked tired and old suddenly. "I don't know, maybe a touch of both."

"Will my coming here start trouble?" she asked.

He took her face in his hands. "My dear Laurel, nothing will keep you from me now. Nothing. One thing you'll learn about me: I may be loud and boisterous, but I'm honest. I'll never lie to you or anyone. Yes, there may be trouble. We can weather it. You and I are McCallisters. We can see it through. I will, however, talk to Ada; Ram, too, I guess." He uttered a mild oath.

"That's another thing that will have to stop," Laurel said stubbornly. "The Indians didn't curse, and the Tatums taught me better than to even think a swear word, and my short stay with the Grants showed me why." Her look softened somewhat when her eyes met a pleased, proud Jeremy's.

"What?" roared Angus. "A wee lass like you telling me I can't drink, and now I can't even swear like a man?"

Hands on hips, Laurel demanded firmly, "It'll be all women in heaven, then?"

Angus's mouth fell open; then he burst into the heartiest laughter Laurel had ever heard. When he finally stopped, he said with a proud look and a tear in his eye, "You, my dear, are indeed a McCallister."

Laurel prepared to move into her family home. Flora cried. Jeremy moped.

It was simple to appease Flora by telling her she'd visit often, and they'd get together to shop and have coffee. But Jeremy was another matter. Laurel wasn't sure how to approach him. He'd grown fond of his charge, that was obvious. How did she feel about Captain Jeremy Grant? She wasn't sure, but she definitely had lost the anger she had felt toward him at the beginning.

At breakfast, the day before she was to move to the ranch, Dusty joined Flora and Laurel. Flora heaped enough bacon and eggs on his plate to satisfy a whole stable of horses. He ate heartily.

"So you're really a McCallister?" he asked.

"Yes. I am Laurel Anne McCallister. My mother was Genevieve Beauforte, of Chicago, and my father is Angus McCallister, of Fort Worth, Texas." She smiled proudly. "It is so comforting to have a past and future."

"I'm real happy for you, Br—, I'm sorry, Laurel."

Laurel touched his hand. "You'll visit me?"

"Sure. But, don't ask me to socialize with Ram Atwood."

"Ram?"

"Yep, he's not too popular."

"Why?"

"He's a wild one. Mixes with the wrong people. I've been doing some detective work, and he's definitely into something other than blacksmithing. He has too much money and too many bad connections. Don't trust him. In fact, if I were you, I'd stay clear of him altogether, if possible."

Laurel bit her lip. "I'll remember that."

Dusty's words haunted Laurel all morning. She wondered if she should call on Melita. Hadn't she invited her to? Would she sincerely help? Could Melita Coopersmith be trusted?

Laurel wondered how Ada and Ram had taken the news of her moving to the ranch. Would there be trouble? What type of reception would she get when she moved in?

When Laurel went up to dress for dinner, a pink chiffon party dress was laid out for her. She shrugged and put it on. If Flora had gone to the trouble of buying it, she'd humor her and wear it.

A few minutes later, Flora appeared and fixed her hair. Flora often helped Laurel braid her hair, but tonight she suggested something different. Scooping up the thick, auburn tresses, she pinned them high and let the curls cascade down Laurel's back. At her ears, Flora used a curling iron to coil a few strands. Laurel gasped when she looked at the results in the full mirror. The light reflected her hair just enough to sparkle the red highlights, giving her a distinctive air. Spinning before the mirror, Laurel found it difficult to recall being Running Brook, clad in buckskin, sleeping in a drafty tepee.

As she descended the stairs for dinner, Laurel was pleasantly surprised to find Jeremy waiting at the foot of the steps to escort her to the dining room. Dressed formally, he looked quite handsome. Love for the Grants poured through Laurel. They were making a fuss for her tonight because they cared. She would truly miss them.

Jeremy stared up at her, as if in awe. Laurel's mouth

curved into an unconscious smile. She did look fine, didn't she? She liked being an attractive young lady. Stirrings within told Laurel she liked Jeremy's look and the fact that he found her lovely. Joy bubbled in her heart and shone in her bright-blue eyes.

Yet when they approached the dining room and Dusty, who stood lounging against the wall, gave her the same look of approval, disappointment overwhelmed Laurel. Dusty, her pal, shouldn't look at her that way. Yet she was an attractive woman, so why should he not? What was the matter with her?

Dusty looked crestfallen when he saw her on Jeremy's arm. Had he hoped to escort her to dinner? Laurel realized she must be careful if she did not want to cause any rivalry between the friends. She smiled at Dusty and took his arm also.

Between the two men, Laurel McCallister made her first public debut, for inside the dining room sat people she did not recognize. She gasped in surprise.

Flora approached and took charge of Laurel, leaving Dusty and Jeremy to stand behind their chairs while Flora took her around the table and introduced her to their many friends and neighbors. One face Laurel recognized: Melita Coopersmith. She sat with an elderly woman whom Flora introduced as Melita's mother, Cora Coopersmith. Laurel expressed delight at seeing Melita again, which seemed to please the woman.

Finally escorted to her seat, Laurel found herself next to Jeremy, who sat at one end of the large table. Across from her sat Dusty, Melita, and her mother. At the far end Flora graced the table's head.

Laurel felt as if she would awake from this dream soon. She'd actually been introduced as *Laurel McCallister*. She was someone!

Jeremy said grace beautifully, and everyone enjoyed a delicious dinner. Laurel felt regal. Laughing within herself, she wondered how these people would react if she ate as she'd eaten when she lived with the Comanche. Silently she asked the Lord to bless Mrs. Tatum for teaching her critical skills that had once seemed unimportant.

Preoccupied with her own dream world, Laurel hadn't thought about Melita and Jeremy. Once the thought crossed her mind, she began watching them to see if one or the other showed any sign of affection. Melita gazed at Jeremy often during her meal, but Jeremy did not look her way at all. He looked mostly at his mother or Laurel. Did he no longer care for the girl he'd planned to marry? Or was he playing games with her? Would Melita resent her because of Jeremy's attentiveness? One thing Laurel knew for certain: She liked Jeremy's attention, and she'd have been hurt had he been attentive to Melita and not her.

For the first time she admitted to herself she was truly fond of Jeremy Grant. Yet this fact did not elate her. What if Jeremy and Melita got back together? They were very close at one time—engaged. Caring for someone meant making yourself vulnerable, and the years with Big Bear had taught Laurel to defend herself from pain.

Unwittingly she turned toward the object of her thoughts. As her eyes met Jeremy's they smiled at each other instantaneously. Such a kind man could not hurt her as Big Bear had. Suddenly trust flowed between them, and all the doubts she'd experienced seemed swept away.

As Laurel glanced at Dusty, all her breezy self-confidence evaporated. He'd caught the gesture and an expression of hurt and disappointment covered his face.

Poor Dusty. Had she falsely encouraged him? Jeremy would think so, yet she had always felt comfortable with her friend Dusty. What right did he have to want more from her? Couldn't he be happy for her if she and Jeremy . . . ? She stopped that train of thought. *Too soon,* she reminded herself. *Don't think along those lines yet. At least wait until you see what happens between Melita and Jeremy.*

After dinner, the guests were shown to the living room for coffee. Some sat, while others milled about, socializing. Laurel stood by the door, allowing the guests an opportunity to convey their best wishes to her and her new family. Despite her light conversation, Laurel kept one eye on Melita and Jeremy. For some reason her interest in them became of paramount concern.

Melita had spent most of her time after dinner introducing her mother to people. Now Laurel noticed Melita's eyes often searched the room. Searching for Jeremy? Did Melita still care for him? Laurel worried. If so, why had she left him for this Ram?

When Jeremy wasn't talking to people, he stood, broad shouldered and handsome, watching Laurel from a distance and smiling his approval whenever their eyes met. She needed his support and was glad for it, even depended on it. Why hadn't she realized before tonight how much she cared for Jeremy?

While an elderly couple told Laurel the story of how they had met and settled in Fort Worth, Laurel's eyes searched for Melita. She finally spotted the woman edging her way through the crowded room toward Jeremy. The way someone constantly interrupted Melita's progress almost amused Laurel. After several frustrated attempts to reach him, the woman became agitated and actually began to ignore the guests who called her name or began to converse with her, in order to reach the fireplace, where Jeremy stood, watching Laurel.

Finally reaching him, Melita tapped his arm and said something that made him laugh. They stood talking. The old couple, possibly tired of Laurel's inattention, had moved on; the local preacher, Reverend Billy Childs, took their place. Yet she kept one eye on Melita, who continued talking animatedly with Jeremy.

She felt her composure weakening. How could Laurel compare with Melita? While she herself was attractive, Melita abounded with beauty, grace, and intelligence. Laurel could barely read and write or carry on a witty conversation. Suddenly her dream world seemed less than ideal.

Yes, people called her lovely. She now had a family, but she still felt inadequate. How could she learn to be smart, like Melita Coopersmith? How could she compete with perfection?

Laurel quickly chastised herself. If Jeremy preferred Melita to her, then so be it. What could she do about it? It was not going to spoil her perfect evening. Pleased with herself for making such a decision, Laurel laughed with the preacher at a comment he'd made. Yet when she saw Jeremy lead Melita outside, a wave of apprehension swept through her, and her stomach clenched tight.

9

This should be the happiest day of my life, thought Laurel. *Yet I've never felt worse. Why?* She sighed and nudged her horse with her heel. Here she rode to her family at last, and who showed up to escort her? Dusty. Why? Because Captain Jeremy Grant had been too busy.

Laurel spurred her horse again. Of course she liked Dusty, but she had wanted Jeremy to escort her. Yes, she was disappointed at Jeremy's disappearing act with Melita last night. She felt momentary panic as her thoughts jumped onward. Where had they gone? What had transpired between them? Had he stayed out too late with Melita? Was that why Flora had made excuses for him?

Laurel, obsessed with her thoughts, had lagged too far behind, and Dusty had halted to wait for her. When she caught up, the man, who had been quiet smiled and commented, "You don't seem happy for a gal who has just discovered her family and is going home after eighteen or more years."

"I *am* happy. I'm just unsure of my reception," she excused herself.

"You mean Ram and Ada?"

"Yes," she replied, yet she knew Angus would not allow them to be impolite to her.

"Or is it Melita and Grant who have you upset?"

"What do you mean?"

"I saw them leave together, too. They're probably engaged again, if I know Grant. He never could resist Melita. She's his Achilles' heel, I fear."

"Achilles' heel?"

"His weakness, so to speak."

"So you think they will end up together?" Laurel asked, heart thumping wildly.

"I never doubted it."

"But what about Ram?"

"Ah, he was just a temporary diversion—probably to make Grant jealous. You see, Jeremy kept prolonging the engagement by postponing the wedding date. I think she just used a different tactic to get him nailed."

"Nailed?" she asked, puzzled by his slang.

"Married."

"Oh, Dusty." She scratched her auburn head. "You confuse me."

"Sorry. I believe Melita used her interest in Ram to get Jeremy Grant jealous enough to finally set a wedding date and keep it."

"Do you think her plan worked?"

"You saw them leave together last night."

"Yes, I did." She stiffened her back and tried to act as though it mattered little to her. "If he's so easily misled by Miss Coopersmith, then he deserves to be—as you called it—'nailed.' "

"Don't worry," comforted Dusty. "If you need anything, just call me."

"Thank you, Dusty." She smiled. Why should Captain Jeremy Grant and Melita spoil her special day?

Drawing up to the ranch house, Dusty helped her dismount. "Well, here you are—home."

"Yes," she murmured, feeling lost.

Laurel spun around her new bedroom. She must pinch herself to be sure she wasn't dreaming. Though it smelled a bit musty, she could see efforts had been made to alleviate that. Curtained French doors that led to a small balcony stood open wide. The room was magnificently large and feminine. Had it always been this beautiful, or had *someone* gone out of the way to please Laurel? Surely not Ada. Her welcome had been stiff and cold, albeit polite. Laurel felt no friendship there.

The furniture, made of light-colored wood, had numerous carvings on the doors and drawers. Laurel ran her hand across the dressing table. Looking at herself in the mirror, she smiled. *How far I've come!* She toyed with her braid and stared at her image. One hand smoothed the blue gingham dress she wore.

What will my future be? Suddenly Laurel felt very alone and vulnerable. She gazed around the lovely room with its pink, ruffled bedspread and pink-and-white gingham curtains. While lovely, everything suddenly frightened her. She gazed at her image in the mirror.

Here I am, but what do I do now? I have a new life. Will I do it justice? What will I make of myself as Laurel McCallister? What if I fail? She shivered, despite the heat of the afternoon. *What if something happened to Angus or Maggie? They are all I have now.* The surroundings were foreign, yet this was her home. But what is home without familiar things? She felt no comfort here.

Her eyes scanned the room for some familiar object and stopped short at a book on the nightstand. She walked over, picked it up, and read its title: *Holy Bible.* She hugged it to herself. The Tatums had gained great comfort from this book, and she'd seen several Bibles in the Grants' home, too. Though she couldn't read as well as some, she drew comfort from the familiar object. She'd never seen this particular book before, yet it was not strange, but familiar, like home.

Replacing the Bible, she stepped out onto her small balcony, and took a deep breath. Fresh air! Her room must have been locked up for some time. She settled herself comfortably in a large rocker in the corner of the balcony and soon fell fast asleep.

For the first time since on the trail from Oklahoma, Laurel's nightmare reoccurred. While different, it was no less frightening. Instead of bloody scalps or dying babies, she had visions of her taunting Indian playmates and the torturous tricks they often played on her. Again, she awoke to her own shrill scream.

Looking about frantically, hoping no one had heard or seen her, she fled inside her room. Surely no one had seen her. Only time would tell if someone had heard her cry.

Once inside, she stopped short. Her hand flew to her mouth to prevent another scream as she faced a figure in the doorway.

Worried eyes scanned Laurel and her surroundings, then looked at her questioningly.

"Oh, Maggie! It's you!" Laurel let out her held breath.

Maggie's eyes demanded an answer.

"I'm sorry, I napped and had a bad dream."

Maggie's form relaxed. Apparently Laurel had a loyal protector. Did she need one here?

Laurel reached out and hugged Maggie. "Oh, how I wish you could talk!"

Maggie broke from the embrace and looked at her with tear-filled eyes. She thumped her chest with her hand while her eyes pleaded with Laurel.

"You?" she guessed. "Maggie? You?"

Maggie nodded happily. She then held her hand gently over her own heart and again coached a response from Laurel.

"Chest?" Laurel asked, but quickly changed her answer when Maggie frowned. *"Heart?"* A half-excited look told her she was close, but not accurate. Laurel sighed, *"Chest . . . heart . . . feelings . . . ,* I know! *Love!"* she cried excitedly.

Maggie smiled broadly, then held up both hands for her to expect another word. She then placed her index finger on Laurel's forehead.

Laurel smiled and took the woman's hands in hers. "I love you, too."

Maggie smiled but seemed still unsatisfied. She scanned the room, and with an excited look, her eyes found the Bible. She motioned for Laurel to sit beside her on the bed while she opened the large, leather-covered book.

The old woman pointed anxiously to the first page.

Laurel squinted to read the words. Luckily, someone had written in neat, large letters. Laurel read aloud: "To Angus and Genevieve: May God bless you on this, your wedding day, and every day hereafter. Love, Mother."

Farther down the page another message appeared: "Born April 8, 1853, Laurel Anne McCallister." Someone had drawn a tree with branches and offshoots from these branches. Maggie pointed to a large branch, and Laurel read the words. "Margaret Anne McGraw—Angus McCallister, June 5, 1800." She looked at the excited Maggie. "Is that you, Margaret Anne McGraw?" Maggie nodded, pointing to the branches stemming from her and Angus McCallister's branch.

Laurel traced each branch with her finger as she read aloud: "Malcolm, born 1802; Donald, born 1804; Mary, born 1807; William, born 1810; Hertha, born 1812; Gordon, born 1815; Angus, born 1817; and Patrick, born 1820."

Laurel pointed to *Angus, born 1817.* "Is this my father?"

Maggie nodded.

"Where are all the other children?" she asked.

Maggie flipped the Bible's pages to the back inside cover and pointed. There Laurel could not make out the entries as well. They were not written as precisely. It appeared to be a record of many deaths.

"Are none alive?"

Maggie shook her head, sadly. Flipping the book back to the front, she pointed to Angus's name.

"Just Angus?"

Maggie frowned and nodded. She flipped through the Bible's pages, then scanned a page before pointing to a word and urging Laurel to read it.

"Father?" Laurel asked.

Maggie nodded definitely, then pointed to Angus's name again.

Laurel thought she understood. "You don't like me calling my father Angus?"

She nodded once.

"All right," agreed Laurel. "I will try to remember." She patted Maggie's hand lovingly. "It will become a habit in no time."

Yet Maggie's troubled look continued. She pointed to her own name, then pointed to herself, again coaxing Laurel.

Laurel smiled. "Yes, Grandmother. I understand."

The woman smiled excitedly and hugged Laurel.

"We are family," said Laurel. "And thank you for showing me our family tree. It's comforting to know where I came from."

Maggie picked up the Bible, kissed its cover, and handed it to her granddaughter. The book Laurel had felt she knew turned out to be a family heirloom. Already, without even having read from it, the book had given her security.

Before departing, Maggie pointed to the large mantel clock on the shelf over the bed and tapped the number six. Laurel knew she would be back then to escort her to dinner.

Bored with exploring her room, Laurel returned to the balcony. Longing to walk around the ranch, she swung her legs over the low rail and headed toward the creek. She toyed with the shallow water, then decided to follow the crooked, winding stream away from the house. As she wandered out of sight of the ranch, she comforted herself with the thought that it would be impossible to get lost if she stayed by the stream.

She crossed the stream several times by stepping on large rocks, but never left it. The sandy area had few trees, but the farther she roamed from the house the thicker the bushes and brambles grew. Her surroundings' serenity calmed her. Perching atop a large rock, Laurel drew up her legs and gazed at the barren yet beautiful area around her. She wondered which direction was Oklahoma, then which direction was the Grants' home. The thought of Jeremy filled her with regret. When would she see him again? Staring up at the blue sky, she hugged her legs. The vision of Jeremy leading Melita through the front door and out into the darkness last night haunted her.

As the sun dipped behind the distant, faded-purple mountains, she realized the time, scrambled off the rock, and headed for the creek she'd followed. She'd crossed the creek so often that when she tried to recall which side she'd begun on, she became confused. Had she crossed it to sit on the rock, or had it been on her side of the creek? Why hadn't she noticed the sun's position before she sat down?

The scenery around her seemed all the same. No distinguishing landmarks helped her note her way. She looked about, bewildered. Soon it would be dark and Laurel knew she had to make a decision. She chose to take the direction away from the sun, a short distance, to see if anything looked familiar. If not, she could quickly go the opposite way.

She rounded a sharp bend in the creek and breathed a sigh of relief. She knew for certain she was heading in the wrong direction, for ahead was a shanty. If she had passed one earlier, she'd have recalled it.

Preparing to spin around and head back, she noticed two horses tied to a tree near the shack and heard loud voices inside. Before she could take a step, a word of the conversation within drifted her way, *Indian*. She paused and squatted, Indian fashion, beside a small bush and listened to the two male voices.

"How many men are riding with the shipment?" queried one.

"Jeb said about a dozen. That's twice as many as before. How do you expect us to grab the haul with that many guarding it?"

"Then we'll hire more men and catch them off guard."

"Where'm I going to get more men?" the gruffer voice whined. "You said yourself we shouldn't let too many in on this. Now that you've got that Indian squaw living here, we'll have that sneakin' army captain and his Indian pal nosing around. I tell you, we ain't going to get away with stealin' another Indian supply wagon."

"You leave *them* out of this! I'll take care of *them!*" the commanding voice answered with such vengeance that Laurel shivered. "Ask Jeb, Bo, or one of the other regulars if they know anyone who can be trusted. Didn't Bo say his brother wanted in to some action?"

"Yeah, but I think he meant gamblin'—he's a bad drinker, too. If you 'member, we decided not to trust him."

"Well, now perhaps we have no choice."

"Aw, we already stole four supply wagons; we'll get caught. How about goin' back to rustlin' cattle? There's talk the railroad will run through Fort Worth by next year or so, and they'll build stockyards right here."

"True, but until then we have to hustle them too far, and our chances of getting caught are even higher. Besides, we're only stealing what rightfully belongs to *us.* Why should our government clothe and feed those savages?"

"How many more will we have to take?" the gruff voice asked with a tired sigh.

"As many as we can, and if you love cattle rustling so much, you'll be happy to hear that the government just bought several thousand head near Dodge City, and they're driving them to the reservations, to be divided amongst the Indians."

"Got the details?"

"No, but I'm working on it."

"Is it still all right for me to live here, or do I have to move now that the squaw's up at the big house?"

"Stay here! She won't nose around this way, and even if she did, you're my right-hand man is all. Nothing strange about the foreman living on the ranch."

"Good. Hey, where you goin'? Want another drink?"

"No. I'm expected for dinner, to meet my new family member."

Laurel heard no more, for she darted for the creek and in

the right direction, as fast as her legs would carry her. If that man saw her and suspected she'd heard anything, she'd be as good as dead.

Stopping for breath, she leaned against a lone cottonwood. Feeling eyes on her, she scanned the area. She gasped. A lone horseman sat a mere fifty feet from her, staring. Shocked, Laurel merely stared back.

10

The man dressed all in black squinted, touched the gold band on his hat, turned his horse, and sped away.

Laurel blinked and breathed deeply. Who was this formidable man? Had it been one of the two she'd heard talking in the shanty? She shivered. If so, had he seen her listening? Did he know she'd heard their plans?

Picking up her skirts, she ran all the way back to the ranch house, climbed back over the balcony, and slid into her room.

Someone had pressed the pink party dress and brought her hot water and towels. After she'd washed and dressed, she sat upon the bed and began unbraiding her hair.

Running the conversation she'd overheard back through her mind, she wondered, *Who were those horrid men?* She must find a way to warn Jeremy. *But how?*

Maggie came in at exactly six and brushed Laurel's hair briskly, then surprised her by not rebraiding it but tying it at the nape of her neck with a pink ribbon. Her auburn hair fell thickly down her back. Laurel gazed at herself in the mirror and decided she liked the hairstyle.

"It's beautiful, Mag— Grandmother. Thank you."

Maggie beamed. The steel gray of her dress highlighted her blue eyes, which danced with pride in her granddaughter. Arm and arm they walked down the long corridor to the dining room.

Angus, seated at the table head, looked up at Laurel with shining eyes. "You do our name proud, lass."

She kissed his forehead. "And I wear the name proudly."

"Sit here." He patted the green velvet chair beside him. Maggie sat across from her. Ada entered next and, smiling coldly, took the seat at the table's foot, across from her husband. One seat remained empty, the chair between Laurel and Ada.

Angus pounded the table with his fists. "Where is your son? Why does he always keep us waiting? Especially tonight, he could have made an effort to be here on time!"

Calmly, as if used to his behavior, Ada remarked, "He came home late."

Angus turned to Laurel. "As soon as—"

The sound of a man clearing his throat made all eyes fly toward the doorway. There, smiling broadly, stood the man in black, who'd stared at Laurel on the trail. His brown eyes sparkled with mischief, and his cheeks dimpled. Laurel stared in amazement. *Not only is this the same one,* she thought, *but he is handsomer than any man I've ever seen.* She could almost understand poor Melita's confusion, having to choose between an absent army captain and this charming young man.

Angus stood. "Ram Atwood, I'm proud to present my daughter, Laurel McCallister."

Ram walked to her chair and bowed. "Pleased to meet you, Laurel. Welcome to Three Gates Ranch." His eyes, still smiling, pierced hers meaningfully, as if to say, *I know it was you, and I know what you heard.*

The words he'd uttered in the shanty echoed through her mind. "You leave *them* out of this! I'll take care of *them!*" Unnerved, she could only nod and smile feebly at him.

Ram took the seat beside her, and immediately a heavy-set woman began setting hot dishes before them.

Laurel welcomed the end of the meal, for she'd been too nervous and upset by Ram's presence to eat. After ushering her into the living room, Ram excused himself. Taking her hand, he bowed again. "A pleasure to meet you, Laurel *McCallister.*"

"Thank you," she answered feebly.

"I apologize. I must hurry off. Business, you know." He watched her, his expression grim.

Laurel felt like saying, "No, I don't know anything!" but instead responded, "I understand."

"We'll ride together one day. I'll show you the ranch. A date?" he asked, changing to his charismatic boyishness. Laurel found herself agreeing, despite herself.

When he'd gone, she tried to shake off his effect on her. Between his looks and his style, a woman didn't have a chance against Ram Atwood. Laurel felt sympathy for Melita.

In the morning, because she felt homesick, Laurel dressed in her white buckskin and moccasins. All the while she dressed and braided her hair she pondered how to get in contact with Jeremy Grant. *Ride to the Grant home?* No. She'd never find it on her own, for there were too many streets and turns to remember. *Send a message?* Probably best, but how? Should she confide in her father? She knew he could be trusted, but he was so loud. Maybe someone would overhear him, for certainly he'd rant and rave. *No.* She must contact Jeremy.

Maggie! She jumped up excitedly as the obvious solution struck her. *Maybe Maggie could get a message to Jeremy.*

She sat at the desk in the corner of the room and poised a pen over the blank paper. Would Jeremy laugh at her childish handwriting? Would he compare her to the intelligent Melita? Laurel shrugged. She had little choice. Jeremy must know what was going on.

Deciding it was best to keep the message short and to the point, she merely printed:

> Jeremy:
> Important that I see you at once. Don't tell anyone except Flora.
>
> Laurel

Folding the paper and hiding it in one hand, she headed for Maggie's room. When Laurel knocked softly on her door, Maggie answered almost at once. Smiling broadly, she pulled her granddaughter into her simply furnished bedroom.

Sitting upon the bed, Laurel handed the missive to Maggie. "Grandmother, can you see that this gets to Jeremy Grant? It's terribly important."

The old woman took the letter with a questioning look.

Laurel didn't want Maggie to worry. "I miss the Grants and forgot to thank Jeremy. I feel dreadful. He helped me, and I never thanked him. It has me worried. Can you help?"

Looking at Laurel suspiciously, Maggie pocketed the paper and nodded briskly as if to say, "Done."

"Thank you." She kissed the old woman. "It means a great deal to me. And now, I'm going to my father's room. He's going to teach me something called checkers."

* * *

Ram's absence at dinner that night was again explained away as business. Laurel felt relieved; his presence confused her because her reactions to him were so ambiguous.

Just after they retired to the living room for coffee, the hired woman, Clarita, announced guests: Jeremy and Flora Grant.

Laurel spun around to face them. Her eyes met Jeremy's and she felt her heart flutter. She smiled at him and greeted Flora with a hug. Had they received her message so soon? Or had they missed her already and merely stopped by?

"How wonderful to see you," she said. "Have you met Ada and my father?" she asked.

"Oh, yes," Flora answered. "I have, though I haven't run into either in ages. It's so nice to see you both again."

Ada and Angus welcomed their guests, and Ada surprised Laurel by becoming the perfect hostess. She asked Clarita to bring coffee and cake and spoke graciously to Jeremy and Flora. Ada seemed warmer than ever before. Who was she trying to fool with her kindness—Angus or the Grants?

Laurel bit her lip. How could she signal Jeremy? Could she manage somehow to get him alone?

She glanced at her father. Angus was ranting and raving about cattle rustlers and how they should be caught and hung. Now Laurel wished that she'd confided in him; maybe he'd be able to help.

She turned to study Jeremy, who was listening raptly. Then her eyes met two anxious gray ones. Flora! She winked knowingly and nodded toward Jeremy with a slight smile. Laurel breathed a sigh of relief. They knew! Jeremy and Flora would help her, but she must remain alert for cues. She folded her hands in her lap and waited.

During an unusual lull in the conversation—for Angus loved company and an audience—Flora addressed Laurel casually: "So, my dear, have you become accustomed to ranch life?"

Laurel smiled. "It's lovely here. I'm sure I'll feel at home in no time."

"We're happy for you, but miss you terribly. The house isn't the same, seems so empty. Doesn't it, Jeremy?" she nudged her son.

"Definitely," he agreed, adding, "Smoky wanders the house, looking for you constantly."

"Oh! I miss him, too!" Laurel cried. "Is he eating well?"

Flora chuckled. "As much as he misses you, he hasn't given up his favorite pastime of eating. He's getting mighty fat, too!"

"What's this?" asked Angus. "Who is this Smoky?"

"Oh, Father, he's the sweetest kitten we found on the way here from Oklahoma. I sort of adopted him."

"Then why isn't he here with you?" he roared, ignoring Ada's gasp.

"We couldn't keep a cat here, Angus!" blurted Ada. "Ram sneezes his head off at just the sight of one."

"Ram won't be anywhere near her room." He turned to Laurel. "You may bring the cat here, if you can keep it out of Ram's way."

Despite Ada's sneer, Laurel clapped her hands together. "Oh, Father, thank you! May I get him tomorrow?"

"Certainly."

Flora held up one hand. "Not so fast, Laurel. I think it's fine for people to take in pets, but only if they can be cared for properly. Let us see if your room is an adequate place for a kitten to be kept. They do need space to run and play, and remember, he will grow."

When the sparkle left Laurel's face, Flora winked. "Let's check this room, Jeremy." Laurel caught the cue and led them to her room.

Jeremy and Flora Grant followed Laurel down the long hall to her door, midway along the corridor. Once inside, with the door closed, Flora relaxed and hugged Laurel affectionately.

"How did you get my message so quickly?" Laurel asked.

"Dusty brought it."

"Please sit down." Laurel seated herself on the bed's edge, so her guests could occupy the two chairs.

Jeremy's eyes scanned the room. He walked to the French doors and opened them. After disappearing through the door for several moments, he returned, closed the doors, and sat in a chair beside his mother. "It's safe to talk. What is it, Laurel? Is something wrong?"

"I don't know where to begin!"

"Keep your voice low and start at the beginning," said Jeremy.

Laurel gulped, folded her hands serenely in her lap, and wet her lips. "I decided to walk and followed the creek. Stupidly, I crossed it so many times that when it became time to return I couldn't remember which way to go. I chose the wrong way and came to an old shanty. Just as I began to turn around and go back, voices stopped me." She had Flora and Jeremy's full attention.

"Two men were discussing Indians. One voice sounded educated and definitely belonged to the leader. They talked about stealing the supplies the government was sending to the reservation Indians. The second man told the leader he'd heard now more men guard it, so he had better get more men to steal it." Laurel's excitement caused her cheeks to flush. Her whisper had grown louder due to her excitement. Remembering, she continued in a lower pitch, "The hired man mentioned that my living here would complicate things, especially with the army captain and

Indian snooping around. He suggested something be done about it."

Flora, still silent, paled, her eyes widened. A look of concern covered Jeremy's face, but he made no comment.

"The leader's words frightened me," Laurel said. "Not so much *what* he said, but *how* he said it."

Flora leaned forward and patted Laurel's hand. "Tell us, dear, and then you won't have to think of it again."

"He said," Laurel imitated the emphasis Ram had used, " 'You leave *them* out of this! I'll take care of *them*.' "

"It's just talk, Laurel. That's the way tough men are out here. You needn't worry," assured Flora.

Jeremy remained silent, as if carefully contemplating all her words. Finally he spoke. "Did they mention each other's names during conversation?"

"No, but they mentioned some of their men, and—"

Jeremy's eyes widened and he cut in, "What were the names?"

Laurel bit her lip gently. "I'm fairly sure one name was a nickname, *Bo,* I think. The other name I can't recall. This Bo has a brother in town, and the leader suggested that they use him. The hired man mentioned that the brother drank."

"Boynton Hobbs," Jeremy stated. "He's been rustling cattle, too."

"Yes," Laurel said. "They spoke of that. The hired man wants to go back to cattle rustling, instead of stealing Indian shipments."

"Did they say anything else that could give me a clue as to who else is involved or what their immediate plans are?" Jeremy asked.

"But I know who the leader is!" she cried, in a loud whisper.

11

Flora and Jeremy stared at Laurel in amazement.

"You know?" Jeremy asked. "Did you see him?" Then shifting to the edge of his chair, he asked worriedly, "Did *they* see *you?*"

Nervously, Laurel told how she'd seen the man dressed in black staring at her. "It frightened me, but not as much as seeing him walk into the dining room that evening."

"Ram?" Jeremy and Flora chorused.

Laurel nodded. "He sat right beside me. I couldn't eat a bite!"

"I can imagine!" sympathized Flora. "And his attitude toward you?"

"He was polite and said all the correct words, yet something about the way he said them makes me suspect he knows I heard them talking."

"Like what?" asked Jeremy.

Laurel sighed. "Nothing critical, really. Just the way he

emphasized certain words and the way his eyes seemed to pierce my mind and pick out the thoughts."

"What do you mean, 'the way he said them'? Give me an example," Jeremy urged.

"Well, he apologized for having to leave by saying, 'I must hurry off. Business, *you know.*' " Laurel tried to imitate the inflection Ram had used on the words.

"That's all?" Jeremy asked.

"Yes."

He sighed with relief. "Laurel, could it have been your imagination?"

She considered this. Then shook her head. "No. He knows. I feel it."

"Stay away from him as much as you can," Jeremy warned.

"He offered to take me riding, to show me the ranch."

"You mustn't go!" Jeremy pounded his fists on the chair arms, reminding Laurel of Angus.

"But what excuse can I give? I can't refuse his hospitality without a valid reason."

Jeremy stood and paced the floor. Finally he stopped before her. "Be careful, then. I'll have Dusty posted to keep an eye out for you."

Flora stood. "We'd better return before someone wonders where we've disappeared to. If you need us for anything, send word quickly. Simply write the word *help* on a paper, and we'll be here."

Jeremy opened the door. "I think we had better keep Smoky for the time being. The room is big, but too confining for a growing kitten. We'll take good care of him."

Laurel felt disappointed but knew he was right. She nodded.

Approaching the living room, Flora spoke loudly enough for all to hear. "Do you think your father would object to our picking you up for church on Sunday? We'd also love to have you for dinner afterwards."

"Maybe Angus would like to come, too?" added Jeremy.

As they entered the living room Angus said, "Church? Me? It would topple over if I set foot in it."

"Why is that, Father?" Laurel sat on the arm of his chair.

He laughed. "People say I'm a devil of a man!"

"Why, I don't believe that," Laurel said, kissing his cheek. "Will you go with me?"

"No," he said kindly. "But you go ahead."

At her disappointed look, he kindly reprimanded her. "Laurel, my love, I've agreed to quit my whiskey and my cussing, but a saint you'll never make of me. There's many a person would say you've already accomplished the impossible."

Laurel smiled. "Thank you, Father."

As Laurel walked Flora and Jeremy to their wagon, she gazed up at the stars. It was a beautiful evening.

Jeremy helped his mother onto the buckboard wagon, then walked with Laurel to the driver's seat. "I hate leaving you here," he said, searching her eyes carefully, "for more reasons than one."

"I'll be fine," she said with more assurance than she felt.

He took her hand. "Be careful," he whispered.

She looked intensely into his concerned eyes. "Are you worried about my safety?"

"Of course I am. Why would you ask such a question?"

"I never had anyone worry about me before. I rather enjoy the feeling."

"Mother also worries about you."

She smiled. "You are both so kind." Laurel hesitated. "Do you suppose my father worries about me, too?"

"I'm sure of it. You haven't told him about Ram?"

"No. I thought about it but decided against it."

"A good choice. We don't want him worrying."

Laurel looked up into his smiling eyes. "Thank you for your concern," she whispered.

He squeezed her hand. "Just be careful. Don't ride with Ram unless you have to, and then . . . ," he broke off. His worried look had returned. "Don't trust him, not for one second. And . . . ," Jeremy hesitated. "And. . . ." He released her hand and quickly jumped up into the driver's seat.

"And . . . ," she prompted.

"And don't be taken in by his charm," he said and clucked to his horses. As the vehicle rolled down the drive, they both waved.

Laurel spent most of the next day playing checkers with her father. She began to love the time spent with him, especially when he told tales about her mother and other family members. As far as she could see, he'd kept his promise about the whiskey, and he hadn't cussed in front of her. Ada had still not warmed up to Laurel, and Laurel could not figure out why. Her father's wife had no reason to dislike her, though Laurel had good reason to dislike Ada. Several times she'd seen Ada offer Angus whiskey, even encourage him to drink. Ada knew of Angus's promise to his daughter. Did Ada like her husband better drunk? Or did she want to chase Laurel away?

Again, Ram was missing from dinner. Relieved, Laurel ate heartily. Her father seemed silent and thoughtful throughout the meal. When the dishes were being cleared, he made an announcement that made matters worse between her and Ada. "Ada, my daughter needs clothes. Take her into town and buy her everything she needs, as soon as possible."

His wife, who'd been drinking from her wineglass, set it

down carefully and glared at him. "But Angus, there's so much to be done here. Surely you would rather Maggie took her."

"My mother can't talk. How can she bargain with merchants?"

"Flora would take me . . . ," Laurel began to offer.

Angus pounded the table and shouted at his wife, *"You* will take her! She is your stepdaughter, and you will do this for me."

"Very well. We'll go tomorrow," Ada said, with her head held low, so Laurel couldn't see her face. Yet when Laurel got up from the table, she caught a look of indignation in Ada's eyes.

The uneventful shopping spree brought Laurel a complete wardrobe of clothes. Dutifully Ada had done a thorough job of outfitting her stepdaughter. Although she never melted into friendliness, Laurel had caught Ada actually enjoying making the feminine selections. Perhaps she had always wanted a daughter to shop for. Yet the older woman held herself politely aloof.

As Laurel entered the dining room for dinner that evening, wearing a blue silk, square-necked dress, she was surprised to see everyone, including Ram, awaiting her.

She looked at her father anxiously. "I'm sorry. Am I late?"

"Not at all. We were merely early." He patted her chair. "Come, sit down. You look lovely." Angus then addressed his wife. "You did well, Ada."

Ram, who stood upon her entering the room, reseated himself as Laurel took her place between him and her father.

"May I say," Ram turned to her, "that you do indeed look lovely. Yet no lovelier than the first day I saw you—a blue cotton frock, wasn't it?"

Laurel felt the color drain from her face. She was too stunned to speak.

"Beauty such as yours," Ram added, with a devilish twinkle in his eyes, "needs no finery. How can one improve perfection?"

"Thank you," she murmured, embarrassed. Had Ada or Angus realized that she'd worn a pink dress the night she first met Ram at dinner? She guessed not, for they both ate, unaware of the comment. *Remain calm,* Laurel scolded herself. After all, she and Ram both knew he'd seen her that day, running alongside the creek. Did he know she'd also heard their conversation? The thought swept away her appetite.

"So," began Angus, "did you get your kitten?"

"No. Jer—Captain Grant thought my room too small to confine a pet."

"Do you miss this cat?" he asked.

"I do. He is such a darling and keeps me from getting lonely."

Angus looked at Ada sternly, and she braced herself, as if ready for an argument on this score. Before Angus could say a word, Ada sprang to the defensive. "Ram cannot have cats in the house! He sneezes and breaks out in a terrible rash! A cat running about would make him miserable!"

Angus looked as if he'd pound the table in anger, when Ram made his surprising comment. "Her room has a balcony. Why can't she keep the cat in her room and use her balcony doors to let it roam whenever it chooses? He can help cut down on our rodent problems in the barn."

Laurel stared at him in surprise. "But won't it bother you?"

He shrugged. "It only happens when I'm in the same room with a cat."

Laurel swung her gaze to Ada. "Then Smoky can come here?"

Ada shrugged sourly.

"Of course he can," roared Angus. "Thank you, Ram, for the excellent suggestion. You will have a roommate, Laurel. Bring him home with you Sunday."

"Sunday?" Ram asked.

"My daughter has been invited to attend church services and have dinner with the Grants."

Ram frowned and concentrated on spearing his food with his fork. "I see. How considerate of them." Suddenly he perked up. "I never did show you the ranch, Laurel. Tomorrow's Saturday, and I can take a few hours off to take you about. Would that be all right, sir?" he addressed Angus.

"About time, I'd say," he muttered, then looked Ram directly in the eyes and shook his fork at him. "Guard her life well, for it will cost you yours if anything happens to my daughter."

Angus's words and Ram's public invitation assured Laurel that she would be perfectly safe riding the perimeters of the ranch with him.

Dressed in a riding suit of royal blue, with shiny, high, black boots, Laurel met Ram at the stable at the appointed time.

Ram rode alongside her and explained each point of interest. He named each outbuilding and explained what function it served. They toured the corrals, where horses pranced and whinnied, as well as the fields, where cattle grazed. Laurel wondered if any of the animals were stolen.

The areas he showed her were widespread, so a good hour had passed before they reached the shanty where

Laurel had overheard the men talking about stealing Indian supplies.

"This is my headman's place. Hey, Sam!" he yelled. "You in there?"

For the first time that morning, Laurel became nervous. Fear knotted inside her. She hoped Sam wasn't in and frowned with disappointment when the door opened to show a grubby, bearded man in disheveled clothing.

He nodded in their direction.

"I'd like you to meet Miss Laurel McCallister," Ram emphasized her last name.

Sam slid his hat off and held it to his chest. "Mighty nice to meet you ma'am."

Laurel merely nodded and felt glad when they rode on. Trotting slowly, Ram managed to continue the conversation. He elaborated the duties performed by Sam, but Laurel hardly heard, for ahead was the very spot she'd first seen Ram—and he, her. A trickle of perspiration ran down her neck.

Ram uttered an oath and spurred his horse ahead. What had he seen? As Laurel kicked her horse to follow, she saw a figure on the ground ahead. Ram jumped from his horse before it had even stopped and ran to the inert form. Laurel could see that it was a man. Was he asleep? Hurt?

She reached Ram's side just as he turned the body over. Laurel stared in shock. The body with the hole through its head was no stranger. She screamed.

"Laurel," Ram's voice sought to calm her. "I need your help. Do you know this man?"

Gasping and crying, Laurel could only nod frantically.

Ram felt for the man's pulse. "He's dead."

Laurel felt a scream rise in her throat, but before she could utter it, Ram shook her gently. "Laurel, who is it? Who is this man?"

12

Laurel turned from Ram, ran toward her horse, mounted, and rode off in the direction of the ranch. Her head pounded so hard she barely heard Ram's pursuit. His words that day in the shanty ran through her mind, *"I'll take care of them."* She shivered, despite the heat of the day, and urged the horse on faster.

Moments later, Ram overtook her, grabbing the reins and stopping her horse. He pulled her roughly from the saddle and stood her up before him. "Are you crazy? Why did you race off like that? Your father'd have my head if you'd fallen off your horse or gotten thrown!"

Laurel's limbs trembled. Ram tried to comfort her by embracing her, but she pulled away.

"Who was that, Laurel?" he asked. She felt sure he knew the man, yet she played his game, for she was tired and scared.

"Dusty, the Indian scout friend who. . . ." Laurel stopped herself from telling him she'd traveled alone with the two men. "A friend of the Grants—and my friend, too."

"I'm sorry," he offered, not sounding remorseful.

Laurel fumbled for her horse's reins. "I must get word to Captain Grant." She spun around to face Ram. "What will we do about . . . him?"

"I'll go back for him," Ram said. "You ride carefully back to the ranch. I'll handle everything."

Laurel ran to her room and threw herself onto her bed. She wept for Dusty and for herself and Jeremy. She was sure she and the captain would be next.

There would be no funeral, for Dusty wished his remains to be returned to his family, for burial with his own people.

Laurel did not go to church or dinner with the Grants the next day, for her heart ached too much, and she imagined the Grants felt the same. According to her father, Ram had notified Jeremy, and he'd come and taken Dusty's body that very day.

The following Saturday a note came from the Grants, delivered by a young Mexican boy, inviting her to church and dinner. Jeremy would pick her up at nine Sunday morning.

That night, as she played checkers with Angus, she asked him what he thought had happened.

"It's hard to say, lass," he said. "Finding men with bullets in them is not an everyday occurrence, yet it happens from time to time. No one ever knows what happened. An argument? A fight perhaps? Could even have been an accident."

"Do you know why he was on the ranch?" she asked.

"Coming to visit you?" he asked slyly.

"No. He was watching out for me."

Angus looked surprised. "I'm sorry, Laurel. I didn't realize your relationship was—"

"He was my friend. That's all."

Her father let out a breath of relief. "Thank goodness. I'd hate to think you'd lost someone whom you were in love with. It's something you never quite get over."

"Did Ram know Dusty?"

"Captain Grant and Dusty were a well-known sight around town. If Ram didn't know him, he at least knew who he was. Especially with Ram taking up with Grant's old girlfriend, Melita. Why?"

"No reason," she fibbed to save him worry. "I was just curious." She pointed to the game board. "It's your move."

Sunday morning, perched upon the seat of the wagon, Laurel gazed at Jeremy. He seemed sullen, as if coming to the ranch brought back unpleasant memories.

Jeremy turned and gave her a slight smile. "Yes, Laurel, I'll miss him."

"Me, too," she said simply.

He stopped the horses and dropped the reins. "Can you tell me anything about what happened, or is it too upsetting?"

"There isn't much to tell, but you're welcome to whatever information I have."

"Please" was all he said.

"Well, Ram was escorting me around the ranch when he saw something and galloped ahead. By the time I'd caught up, he was already turning over a body. When I saw who it was, I panicked and went to pieces."

"That's it?"

"Yes. Except I wonder about a few puzzling things."

"Like?" he urged.

"Like why did Ram insist I tell him who the man was, when I'm almost sure he knew Dusty."

"Of course he knew who Dusty was. We had our horses shod by Ram just a few months ago."

"Then why did he ask me who he was?"

Jeremy shook his head. "I don't know, unless he had something to do with Dusty's death and acted dumb to throw you off the track."

"That's what I thought, because he did mention you and Dusty that day to his friend in the shanty. Do you think he was testing me? To see if I'd show that I knew that he knew who Dusty was, because I'd listened to the conversation?"

Jeremy shook his head and smiled. "Whoa, you've really thought about this!"

"Too much, probably, huh?" Her brow became furrowed.

"Maybe. What else puzzles you?"

"The place where we found him was exactly where I first looked up that day and saw Ram staring at me. Do you think that's significant?"

Jeremy picked up the reins. "Anything and everything is significant where Ram Atwood is concerned." He clucked the horses into movement.

Laurel's first time in church held her in awe. While small, the building also felt familiar and sacred. Before the service began, Jeremy explained in a whisper that it was also used for a schoolroom during the week. The teacher's desk had been pushed aside and covered with a white cloth. A candle holder upon the linen-topped desk held six flaming white candles, giving it a ceremonious appearance. A wooden podium had been placed at the middle front, and the Reverend Billy Childs took his place behind it.

The church filled to capacity. Several times Laurel had begun counting the people, but she kept losing track each time Jeremy leaned close to explain something. She guessed there were nearly forty people there.

An elderly woman with a large flowered hat played a piano at the rear of the room. Everyone sang a catchy tune. Laurel didn't know the song, but hummed and tapped her toes. She dared not gaze up and stare at Jeremy, though she appreciated the sound of his singing. She hadn't thought Captain Jeremy Grant the singing type, yet he sang beautifully. Laurel felt disappointed when the happy tune ended.

Laurel's attention was drawn to a slight commotion two rows ahead of them. A woman entered, and everyone made room for her. Flora nudged Laurel and whispered, "Melita. Always late."

Laurel noticed Melita's violet dress and smiled to herself. She no longer felt inferior to Melita where clothes were concerned, thanks to her father. Her own pink, ruffled dress, complete with a bustle, looked every bit as stunning as Melita's. Laurel gazed around the room and felt fortunate indeed. Most of the women were dressed as she had been before Angus's generosity. Homespun cottons were nothing to be ashamed of; the women wore them proudly. Laurel almost wished she'd worn one of her cotton frocks, for she thought she could better relate to the women who wore them than she could to Melita and her sophistication.

The Reverend Billy Childs dedicated the service to Dusty and told them not to mourn for him, for Dusty was with his God in heaven. Laurel wondered how Billy Childs could know that. The Tatums had given her the impression that everyone would be judged when the world ended, and God would decide who would enter heaven or hell. If that were true, how could Billy Childs be *sure* Dusty was already in heaven? She must remember to ask Flora or Jeremy.

After the service, as they stood by the wagon, Melita

called out to Jeremy. They turned, and she caught up to them, greeting everyone cordially.

"I'm sorrry to hear about your friend, Jeremy," she said sweetly. "Do you know what happened?"

Jeremy frowned at her. "No, but I intend to find out."

"If I can be of any help . . . ," she began.

"You mean that?" Jeremy asked.

"Of course," she purred.

"Thank you, I may take you up on that offer. Later." He helped Flora and Laurel into the wagon, jumped up himself, and flicked the reins, to move the horses toward the Grant home.

Later that evening, riding back to the ranch with Jeremy, Laurel gazed at the twinkling stars.

"Make a wish!" he exclaimed.

"What?"

"Look! A falling star. Make a wish! Quickly."

Laurel's mind raced frantically. What did she want that she didn't already have? Safety. She wished that their lives were not in danger.

"Did you wish?" he asked.

"Yes. Does the falling star mean it will be granted? Is that a sign from God or something?"

Jeremy laughed. "No. Absolutely not. In fact, Billy Childs would lecture me for seven Sundays if he heard me telling you to wish on a star."

Laurel looked at Jeremy with puzzlement. "Why?"

"Wishing on a star is sort of folklore. Not true, just fun. And if your wish comes true, it's coincidence."

"Oh-h-h," Laurel sighed disappointedly. "I wish it *would* come true."

"I'm sorry," he said sincerely. "I forget that you don't know these things . . . and take them literally." One hand left his reins and lifted her chin. "There's still hope for your wish, you know. You can take it to Someone who *will* grant your wish."

She looked at him hesitantly. "More folklore?"

"No, the honest truth. Have you forgotten God and prayer? Turn your wish into a prayer."

"I don't think I've ever had a wish or prayer granted," she confessed.

"Oh, I'll bet you have. Perhaps it came much later, and you'd forgotten you'd asked. What about finding your family?"

"I can't recall ever asking God for that," she said.

"No? Are you sure?"

"Yes."

"You never felt lonely and asked God to help you to feel better or something?"

"Well—yes," she said hesitantly.

"Then God answered—gave you your wish."

"Before I'd fall asleep," she said excitedly, "I'd ask God to help me feel as if I belonged. I'd ask for someone to love me. Yes," she averred, "God did answer my prayer. Not exactly what I'd asked for, but better."

Jeremy stopped the wagon and turned to her. She saw his eyes sparkle in the moonlight.

"Did you never have anyone love you before you found Angus?"

"Just my best friend, Singing Bird. She's somewhere on the reservation."

"What about your Indian mother?"

"Yellow Moon? She was kind most of the time, but it wasn't the same. She didn't protect me from Big Bear; I guess she feared him, too. I saw Yellow Moon do things that kept me from ever wanting to get closer to her."

"Like what?" he asked.

"Things I've never told anyone, even Dusty."

"You don't *have* to tell me," he said softly.

"I think I'd like to. Maybe the nightmares would end."

He took her hands in his. "Then tell me."

"Big Bear took a second wife when I was about five. Yellow Bird hated it when the other wife, Flower, became with child. Because of envy, she tried several times to cause Flower to lose her baby. One day I watched Yellow Bird trip Flower as she carried a pot of water. Flower lost her baby.

"The next time Flower conceived, all Yellow Bird's attempts failed, and the baby survived. I was thrilled to have a baby brother. Then, the very day of his birth, Yellow Moon smothered him. She thought no one saw. How could I love a woman who could kill a helpless baby?"

Jeremy patted her hands. "You're trembling. You don't have to tell any more. I understand."

"Thank you for listening," she said, feeling a bit embarrassed, as if she'd burdened him with too much of her life.

"And God has also answered the part of your prayer about sending someone to love you, because now you have many who love you."

She looked up at him. "I do?"

He smiled. "If I don't get you home, your father won't love me too much, will he?"

Jeremy gently moved the wagon forward. When they reached the ranch house, he helped Laurel down and walked her to the door. "I want you to be very careful. Stick close to your father, if possible. Don't trust Ram or Ada. If you need help, I've arranged to have Manuel available. Maggie knows how to contact him." He paused and said sadly, "Just as she knew how to find Dusty."

"Then you'll come right away?"

"I won't be here for a few days. That's why I'm so concerned. I'm riding to Fort Sill to get help in stopping Ram and his friends."

"How long will you be gone?"

"I hope only a week." He slapped a knee suddenly. "And I forgot your surprise!" He returned to the wagon and came back with a small wooden crate covered with a cloth.

"What is it?" Laurel asked, gazing at the crate in puzzlement.

"Look." Jeremy folded one end of the cloth so she could peek inside.

"Oh!" she gasped. "Smoky! With everything happening, I'd forgotten him! Thank you, Jeremy!" She leaned forward to kiss his cheek, but Smoky and his cage blocked the way. Jeremy quickly set the crate down, and their embrace fell into place naturally.

It took every bit of Laurel's good sense to pull away from the strange sensations that coursed through her. No contact with another person had ever made her feel this way. Naturally she longed to cling to Jeremy and squeeze him tight.

Later, curled beneath her blankets with Smoky, Laurel wondered if her good sense had proved best. What would it have felt like to be squeezed tightly by Jeremy Grant? Goose bumps made her snuggle deeper within her covers. Had Jeremy felt anything?

A sudden noise broke into her romantic thoughts. She turned quickly toward the sound. The French doors! Even Smoky's ears twitched toward the noise. The moonlight brightened the room just enough to allow her to see the doorknob turn slowly. Had she locked the doors? Laurel's heartbeat seemed to rock the entire bed.

Footsteps sounded, moving away, and the thump of someone leaping over the balcony filled her ears.

Clutching Smoky to her chest, Laurel shivered. *Who had tried to get into her room? Why? Would the intruder try again?*

13

A cool morning breeze caressed Laurel's face, causing her to awake in alarm. The first sight that met her eyes was the open French doors. She sat up quickly, searching for Smoky. Temporarily blinded by bright sunshine, she swung out of bed, but could only stand, frozen, on the bare floorboards. Shielding her eyes, she gazed out. Suddenly a gray streak burst through the doors and skidded to a stop at her feet.

Smoky! She knelt to scoop him up. He purred a greeting. But who had let him out? She walked onto the balcony and all her built up tension came out in an uncontrollable laugh. "Grandmother," she said between giggles, "whatever are you doing on the balcony floor?"

There before her, Maggie lay on her stomach, swinging a piece of red yarn. Slightly embarrassed, the older woman stood and brushed herself clean. She shrugged, patted the cat, and walked into the bedroom.

Laurel followed, still giggling. "I'm glad you like Smoky, Gram."

Maggie nodded with a smile.

"Perhaps you could knit him a few toys." Laurel set Smoky down beside dishes of water and food. "I see you fed him, too."

Maggie nodded, stroking the kitten's back.

"Gram, did you try my balcony door from the outside last night, to see if I had locked it?"

Maggie shook her head, her eyes questioning.

"It was probably Ada. Pay it no mind," Laurel added lightly. She didn't want Maggie worrying. "Give me two minutes, and I'll have breakfast with you," Laurel threw the words over her shoulder as she hurried to dress.

When she returned to her room after her breakfast, Laurel opened the door and out flew Smoky. He scampered down the long hall and Laurel scurried after.

Reaching the living room, Laurel looked about her. *Where did that cat go? If I don't find him, or if Ada or Ram finds him first. . . .* Laurel dared not finish the thought.

A long hall ran along the opposite side of the house—probably, thought Laurel, where Ada and Ram's rooms were. She peered down the hall, and there, near one of the closed doors, pranced Smoky, stalking a housefly. Laurel reached out and grabbed him just as he prepared to spring on the insect. She managed to stiffle his meow of disappointment. As she turned to sneak back to her room, voices caused her to freeze.

Ada's words floated through the closed door. "So what? Angus has every right to change his will. Why are you so concerned?"

"Mother, his daughter will inherit everything!"

Ram's voice! Laurel bit her lip, remembering the trouble

her listening in on him caused the last time. Yet her feet refused to carry her from the door.

"Angus wouldn't do that!" argued Ada. "He's a good man. He said he wouldn't, and I believe him!"

"You discussed this with him? Then you knew he'd sent for his lawyer!" Ram demanded.

"We discussed it last night. He said it was necessary to make a new will now that he knew Laurel was alive. I agree. She is, after all, his daughter."

"She'll get the ranch, I bet. What, my sweet, gullible mother, do you think you'll get for all your trouble?"

"Trouble? What trouble? Angus treats me fine. I live in a nice home and want for nothing. I never would have survived if he hadn't married me and helped me rear you."

"And you've been an excellent wife and deserve better. Just what does he plan to give you?"

"Half."

"Half?" Ram asked mockingly. "Half of what?"

"Half of all his money."

"What about the ranch?" Ram yelled.

"She gets the ranch and the other half of the money."

Ram swore a mild oath, his voice closer to the door. "Why did his daughter have to show up and spoil everything?"

"I'm satisfied, Ram," exclaimed Ada. "Do you have any idea how much money Angus has? We won't need this old ranch!"

"How much . . . ," began Ram, then he stopped mid sentence. Laurel's throat tightened. Why had he stopped talking?

When Ram began sneezing, Laurel fled, squeezing Smoky tightly to her chest. Up one hall, through the living room, and down the other hall, she scurried until she finally stood before her own door. Looking about, she saw no one and silently slipped into the bedroom.

"Oh, Smoky, you almost did us in!" she murmured, kissing his head. "But we're more hated here than I'd thought. Whatever will we do? I'm afraid we're in more danger now than before. We must obey Jeremy and stick close to Angus."

Locking Smoky safely in, she walked to her father's room, thinking he might enjoy a checker game. But when she prepared to knock, she heard voices. She listened momentarily; through the thick wood, she could only hear a strange man's voice. *His lawyer, probably*, she reasoned. *He's changing his will just as Ram said.*

Returning to her own room, she worried and paced. *This will never do. I'll go for a walk. I won't go far, just get some fresh air.*

Leaving Smoky curled up in a chair, fast asleep, she closed the French door behind her, swung her legs over the balcony rail, and dropped down—right into Ram's arms!

"Excuse me!" she cried pushing away from him, but his strong arms kept her against him.

Finally loosening his hold, he laughed. "Where are you going in such a hurry? I've had many women chasing after me, but none has ever thrown herself at me quite so boldly!"

Laurel stamped her foot. "I was *not* throwing myself at you!"

"You needn't protest so fiercely. I was teasing." A swath of wavy hair casually fell on his forehead. He smiled boyishly. "If you're going for a walk, may I join you?"

Laurel thought him arrogant, boorish, and rude. She no longer cared to be polite. "I think not," she spat and turned to walk along the creek.

He grabbed her elbow, bringing her back to face him. His phony smile faded. "Why do you dislike me?" His menacing eyes bored through Laurel. She no longer saw the handsome, charming Ram, but a wild, desperate man. "That first day I saw you by the creek, where were you coming from?"

Laurel shrugged his hand off her elbow and pretended to smoothe imaginary wrinkles from her yellow dress, gaining her time to think. "A walk," she answered simply.

"You were coming from the same direction I was. You went as far as the shanty didn't you?" he demanded.

"Yes," she admitted innocently. "I saw a shanty, decided I'd wandered too far, and turned around and headed back. Why should that concern you? Are you hiding something?"

"Why do you dislike me?"

"You're conceited and arrogant."

"Let me tell you something, Laurel. I've been charming women my whole life. I've yet to find one I couldn't charm. Until you, that is. What makes you immune? Have you heard something about me?"

"As a matter of fact, I have." Laurel's mind raced to invent something.

"What?" he demanded fiercely, grabbing her elbow again.

"Let go of my arm," she demanded, "or my father will hear of this. You have no right to touch me." Ram dropped her arm promptly. "You don't scare me, Ram Atwood. I have my father's protection. *You can't harm me.*"

"What did you hear about me?" He scowled.

"Melita told Flora Grant that you had a wild streak that she thought untameable. That's all I heard."

"And you hate me for that?" he asked.

"I didn't begin hating you until this afternoon. You have no right treating me this way."

Ram dropped his arms and sighed. "You're absolutely right. I don't know what got into me. Will you forgive me?" He looked at her sadly, switching to his boyish charm.

"Yes, but don't let it happen again." She again turned to walk beside the creek.

"Can't we be friends?" he called.

"All right, we're friends," she called back. "Good-bye." Laurel disappeared around the first bend of the creek.

She ran to her rock and perched atop it. Breathing deeply to relieve her tension, she wondered, had she gotten the best of Ram Atwood? Did he believe her story about turning around when she came to the shanty? Despite her predicament, Laurel felt elated, because she guessed Ram's new plan: Charm the rancher's daughter, marry her, and inherit it all. Perhaps it was not such a bad situation. If she played her part correctly, it would keep her alive—at least until Jeremy returned. *I mustn't act too anxious to be courted by Ram, or he'll be suspicious,* she cautioned herself. *If I suddenly fall for his charm, he'll know my game. He knows I dislike him, so my conversion must be slow.* Laurel hugged her knees, suddenly frightened. This was not a game, this was real and dangerous. She closed her eyes and prayed for God's help and protection.

The next two days went as Laurel predicted, and she played mouse to Ram's cat. Did she measure herself properly, not giving in or holding back too much? To be on the safe side, she obeyed Jeremy by sticking close to her father, whose company she'd grown to love. He seemed to love her more each day; Laurel thrived on that fatherly love and loved Angus McCallister dearly in return.

Playing with Smoky, after breakfast one morning, Laurel was interrupted by a knock. She opened her door a tiny crack so Smoky would not dart out and found Ada standing stiffly before her.

"Excuse me. Melita Coopersmith is here to see you. Will you see her in the living room or here?"

"She's here to see *me?*" Laurel asked, surprised.

"Yes."

"I'll see her here," Laurel replied.

While Ada went to get Melita, Laurel dashed around the room, straightening her belongings. She neatened her hair before her mirror and pushed Smoky out onto the balcony. Smoothing the front of her blue cotton dress, she puffed up the lacy sleeves and waited for Melita.

Laurel answered the knock immediately, invited the stylishly dressed woman into the bedroom, and offered her a seat.

Melita smiled sweetly and gazed about the room. "A lovely room for a lovely lady."

"Thank you. How may I help you?" she asked, not sure if she should trust this woman, who Laurel felt still wanted Jeremy Grant.

Removing the plumed hat that matched her mint-green silk dress, Melita spoke softly, "Actually, I thought perhaps I'd come to help you."

Laurel looked at the bright-haired woman in puzzlement. "I don't understand."

"You see," Melita continued, removing her white gloves, "I figured by now you needed a friend."

"A friend?"

"Yes. It must be difficult coming here from Oklahoma and knowing so few people. Ada isn't the warmest person, and Maggie can't speak. I thought you might need a female to talk to. Flora seems to think highly of you, so I decided to offer my friendship. Will you accept it?"

Laurel studied Melita's eyes carefully. The blond woman's eyes didn't waver but returned Laurel's intent gaze evenly. Melita Coopersmith passed the old Indian test of eye contact, but a shiver passed down Laurel's spine. Something didn't add up here; should she trust her?

"I'll accept your friendship, *if* it's indeed sincere." Laurel's glance became sharp.

Suddenly, Melita's eyes filled with tears, and she broke eye contact. She drew out a handkerchief and held it to her nose. "I'm sincere, but not truly sincere!" she cried, more tears flowing.

Laurel dropped to her knees before Melita. "Whatever is the matter? And how can you be sincere but not truly sincere?"

"Ram sent me, but I would have come anyway. I had planned on it. He wants me to—" she broke into tears again.

"Melita," pleaded Laurel, "please calm down. Whatever the trouble is, we can work it out together. Don't cry." Laurel felt totally helpless.

Finally, Melita blew her nose and composed herself. "I'm sorry, Laurel. Can you bear with me?" When Laurel nodded, she continued. "Please answer one question first. When I know where you stand, I can tell you more."

"Ask me anything," Laurel said, sitting on the sofa beside her.

"It's extremely personal, but I need an honest answer. It's important, otherwise I wouldn't think of asking—"

"Ask. It's fine." Laurel assured her.

After nervously playing with her handkerchief, Melita looked into Laurel's eyes and asked, "Are you in love with Ram?"

14

"What?" Laurel felt stunned by the question.

"Are you interested in Ram, romantically?" Melita asked.

Laurel pondered her answer. If she said no, and Melita told Ram, she would have given herself away. If she said yes, she'd be lying. Could she trust Melita? If Melita did tell Ram that she wasn't romantically interested, Laurel reasoned, it wouldn't matter this early in the game anyway. So she decided to be truthful, "No."

Melita sighed with relief. "Yet it took you so long to answer. Are you sure?"

"There were other reasons for my hesitation," Laurel explained. "May I ask why you wanted to know?"

"Certainly," Melita said anxiously. "You see, I'm hopelessly in love with Ram. When I say *hopelessly* I mean just that. I know Ram is a charmer and a manipulator, but I love him anyway. I can't help myself. I realize he doesn't return my feelings, he uses me. But I don't care, as long as it puts me close to him." She shook her head. "It's probably difficult for you to understand, but that's how I feel.

"I can't ignore what he wants to do now. *Because* I love him, I have to keep him from doing this." Her expression darkened with an unreadable emotion.

Melita dabbed at her damp blue eyes. "For some time I've been reporting Jeremy Grant's army business to Ram. It never actually seemed to harm anyone, but it made me important to Ram. I love the Grants, but I told myself my spying didn't hurt them.

"Jeremy wrote so much in his letters, and I passed them all on to Ram. When Jeremy was home, I even stooped so low as to go through his desk and papers for Ram. If Jeremy had ever set a wedding date, I wondered if Ram would have made me marry him. Even now I'd do anything to be near Ram. He has some type of strange hold on me, I know, but I can't resist him.

"Dusty's death woke me up. I'm not sure, but I think Ram may have had something to do with killing Dusty." Melita's tears flowed down her fair cheeks again. "It all happened because of information I passed on to him. Though I can't change what happened to Dusty, I can keep it from happening again.

"Today Ram had the nerve to ask me to persuade you to like him. Your father changed his will, leaving the ranch to you. Ram plans to marry you for the ranch. If you don't cooperate, he plans an accident for you." Melita dabbed at her eyes again. "I never realized how brutal Ram was. I didn't think anyone would be killed!"

"What you are telling me, Melita, is that if I don't marry Ram, I'll die."

"Yes."

"What do you suggest I do?" Laurel asked. "I have no intention of marrying Ram Atwood."

"I wouldn't tell him that yet. We need time."

"Tell me, what exactly did Ram expect you to do by visiting me today?" Laurel asked suspiciously.

"He wanted me to tell you how wonderful he was and that he and I are just friends. He also wanted me to say unpleasant things about Jeremy Grant, for he wonders if you have interests in that area. I think Jeremy is in love with you, but I didn't tell Ram that."

"Why do you think that?" Laurel asked, her heart pounding hopefully.

"The way he looks at you, protects you, and defends you."

"Actually," Laurel said, sweeping aside all secrecy, "your spying on Jeremy for Ram is the only thing I didn't already know. I've been dodging Ram all week. I don't know how much longer I can play cat and mouse." Laurel studied Melita carefully. "What will you do?"

"Me? I'm not sure yet. Trust me, though, I won't help him hurt others. I love him and must make him understand he can't manipulate people. I'll find a way to deal with Ram."

"Melita, if you're in love with Ram, how do I know I can trust you?" Laurel asked. "He may charm you into telling him I have no intention of marrying him."

Melita shook her head. "You'll have to trust me, I guess." The beautiful woman smiled mysteriously and left.

Misgivings overwhelmed Laurel. Had she done the right thing? Opening the French doors, she walked out onto the balcony. As she breathed in the fresh air, she thought about a walk. Yet hadn't Jeremy instructed her to avoid danger by staying near Angus? *Angus! I'll ask my father to walk with me.* Then it dawned on her; she'd never seen her father walk!

Hadn't he always been in the dining room before her and always been in a chair, awaiting their checker games?

Momentary panic overcame her. In her selfishness, she'd never asked after his health. She'd purred just like Smoky over his concern for *her*, yet she'd never thought to ask about him. Guilt at her own thoughtlessness washed over her. Her father could be a cripple or invalid, and she didn't even know it.

Smoky jumped over the balcony railing with something in his mouth and scampered into the bedroom and under the bed. Laurel groaned. Suppose it was a dead mouse or something! Reluctantly she crawled under the bed after the mischievous kitten.

Grabbing Smoky and pulling him out, she pried the object from his mouth.

"Gracious, Smoky," she laughed. "Someone meant well by giving you a juicy hunk of beef, but whoever it is doesn't know how to feed a cat. You'll only eat small chunks of meat."

Smoky sniffed after the beef and meowed.

"Yes, you may have it, after I break it up for you." She kissed his forehead. Walking to his dish, she stooped and began tearing the meat into small, bite-sized pieces. "What's this?" she said aloud, pulling out a large glob of white powder buried within the meat cube. "No!" she yelled and swatted Smoky away from the dish he'd approached with anticipation.

Laurel took the dish away, placed it inside her upper dresser drawer, and closed it. She'd figure out later what to do with it. Perhaps the substance was harmless, but the thought that Ram or Ada might poison the cat remained uppermost in her mind.

For the time being Smoky had better stay inside the room and only go out with her or Maggie. Locking him in, she walked to her father's room. She had to make things right with Angus McCallister.

A boisterous invitation to enter followed her special knock. "Good morning, Daughter." He smiled at the sight of her.

"Good morning, Father." For once Laurel took the time to study him carefully. He sat with a blanket on his lap. Nothing unusual about that.

"The checkerboard is in the cupboard. You caught me unprepared this morning, or are you early?"

"I'm very early, and I didn't come to play checkers. I came to see you. I mean really *see* you." She sat in the chair opposite the small table before him and took his wrinkled, crooked hands in hers. "I've been a selfish daughter, basking in the love and attention you've been showering on me. Until this morning, it never dawned on me that I haven't returned that concern."

"Nonsense," he roared. "You've been the perfect daughter."

"Father, why have I never seen you walk? Are you able? All this time, I've never given it a second thought. I feel terrible."

Angus surprised Laurel by roaring with laughter.

Frustrated with his finding humor in something she felt serious about, she became angry and with arms akimbo demanded, "And what is so funny?"

"I'm sorry, Daughter," he said, trying to stifle his laughing. "Your concern isn't a laughing matter, yet I find myself the object of the joke, not you."

"Whatever do you mean?"

"Had it ever occurred to you that I tried to hide my state of not-so-well-being? A number of times your concern came close to making me disclose my secret." He became more serious. "It just struck me funny that I'd not succeeded.

How foolish I've been to even try to keep it a secret. I guess I didn't want you to know how helpless and feeble your father actually is. How can you possibly feel protected and safe in this world, when your only protector is a feeble, crippled old man?"

"What foolishness," she said, hoping he didn't realize how close to home his statement hit, for that was exactly how she felt. "What's wrong with you?"

"Nothing terribly dramatic. Years of drinking have made me weak, and I've a severe case of gout. I can walk, slowly, with a cane and Ada's help." He sighed, and his eyes filled. "Your father is weak and helpless. I'm sorry."

"If only I'd been able to return to you sooner," Laurel thought aloud.

"That might have helped my condition, but that isn't how it was meant to be."

She rose and hugged the man. "I don't love you any less. You shouldn't have tried to hide it."

Wiping the tears from his eyes, he said roughly, "We all have some vanity. . . . Now get that checkerboard!"

In the hall, returning to her room, Laurel bumped into Maggie.

"Gram, did you give Smoky a large hunk of beef?"

Maggie shook her head, and as usual a worried look followed.

Laurel decided it was time to confide in her grandmother and ushered her into the bedroom. Smoky stretched from his perch atop the highest dresser, where sunshine spread over him. He rolled onto his back, basking to the fullest extent.

Without disturbing Smoky, Laurel removed the food dish from the drawer and handed it to Maggie.

Maggie poked at the white powder and smelled it. She shook her head and looked at Laurel questioningly.

Laurel shrugged. "I don't know what it is or who gave it to him."

Maggie became irritated and pounded her fists, as she usually did when her inability to speak frustrated her. Luckily, she pounded them on the bed, and they made no sound.

Knowing how she felt, Laurel went to the desk and took a pen and piece of paper and brought them to her grandmother. Maggie grabbed them and wrote furiously. Laurel could barely read the words. The gist of the message was that Laurel should guard Smoky until they found out who was responsible.

Laurel agreed. "But isn't it possible that hunk of meat wasn't meant for Smoky? Perhaps Ada or Ram is trying to discourage rats or mice in the stable, and Smoky intercepted the meat."

Maggie shrugged and wrote: *They never use meat on rats or mice.*

"Will you help me take Smoky out, when necessary?"

Maggie nodded, then her eyes lit up. She'd remembered something. Fishing in her pocket, she pulled out an envelope. Handing it to Laurel, she left the room, carrying the dish with the beef.

With pounding heart, Laurel hoped the message was from Jeremy and that he'd returned. As she tore open the envelope she smiled to see his masculine writing.

Strangely, he only said to meet him by the rock along the creek tonight at eight o'clock sharp.

Completely absorbed in thoughts of Jeremy Grant, Laurel managed to get through dinner and Ram's advances and invitations. Pleading a headache, she excused herself early and paced her room until seven-thirty. Then she chose a ruffled powder-blue dress, to match her eyes, and brushed her hair, letting it fall loosely about her shoulders, the way Melita wore hers.

As a final touch, she sprayed her neck with perfume and pinched her cheeks to give them color. Satisfied with her appearance, she kissed the sleeping Smoky on the head and quietly slipped from the room, using the French doors.

When she swung her legs over the balcony, she recalled the last time she'd done so and had fallen into Ram's arms. What would she do if he appeared now? She thanked God that she saw no one and ran along the creek, wondering if Jeremy was already there. Would she have to await him in the dark? She silently thanked God for the quarter moon that helped light the way.

She approached the rock cautiously, for she didn't see anyone and the darkness unnerved her.

Rustling behind her caused her to jump. "It's me, Laurel," a familiar voice sounded from the path behind her. The moon caught Jeremy's face, and Laurel ran to him in relief.

Their embrace seemed natural, and both seemed reluctant to end it.

Jeremy tenderly gazed into her eyes. His eyes shone brightly in the pale light. "I missed you," he whispered.

"I missed you, too," she whispered breathlessly. Then she pulled away, suddenly unsure of her emotions.

"Laurel," he said sternly, "I want you to pack your things and come stay with Flora and me until this matter with Ram is settled. Your life may be in danger."

15

"My life may be in danger?" Laurel laughed. "But you knew that before you left for Fort Sill." *Why the sudden concern?* she wondered.

"Yes, but more so now. I spoke to Melita, and she said—"

"You spoke to Melita, too?"

"Why, yes. She stopped by this afternoon. Did you speak to her?"

Laurel nodded. The moon caught her hair's red highlights, accentuating the waves that fell loosely over her shoulders. "What did she tell you?"

"She has agreed to help set up Ram so the army can arrest him."

"Can we trust her?"

"At this point we don't have much choice. I brought six men back with me, and they're just waiting to get enough proof to nab Ram Atwood and put him away for a long time."

"Did Melita tell you how she had spied on you for Ram?"

He looked down, embarrassed. "She confessed everything. She cried—" he broke off.

"I guess," said Laurel, "our conversations were pretty much the same then. Did she tell you of Ram's plans for me, since he discovered my father changed his will?"

"Yes," his face hardened. "I don't want him even close to courting you, for whatever reason. Don't forget, you're only good to him as his wife or . . . dead."

"You mean he may decide the latter would be faster and easier?"

He nodded. "Get your things together. I'll wait."

She looked up at him and felt the warmth of true concern, yet she couldn't obey. "I can't leave my father and grandmother. Is there no other way?"

Thoughtfully he paced before her.

"Didn't Melita say she'd help set up Ram? Perhaps she can do that quickly. I can dodge him a little longer," she pleaded.

Jeremy took her into his arms and rocked her gently. "I don't want him anywhere near you," he whispered.

Laurel looked up at him and asked, "Why?"

Squeezing her hard, he whispered in her ear, "Because I love you."

Laurel pulled away in surprise and stood gaping at him. Within moments his lips were pressing hers in the most wonderful expression of affection Laurel had ever experienced: her first kiss. When it was over, her knees wobbled, and she embraced him again, more to keep herself upright than out of affection—though she felt plenty of that, too.

Shyly, she looked into his clear, gentle eyes. "I love you, too."

His embrace tightened. He whispered, his breath hot against her ear, "Then come with me tonight."

Pulling away, she held him at arm's length. "Give me a

little more time. I'd have to explain everything to my father. I couldn't just leave him. He can't walk, you know?"

"Not at all?" Jeremy asked.

"Hardly. He walks some with a cane. He needs me."

Jeremy sighed. "I don't know what to do. I've never been more worried about anyone than I am about you."

"I promise to be careful, and if need be, I'll send for you."

"All right," he said, "but I don't feel right about leaving you here."

Laurel gazed into his large concern-filled brown eyes. With her own blue orbs she silently begged to be kissed again.

She got her wish.

When Laurel returned to her room, she flopped down upon the bed and sighed. "Welcome to your new life, Laurel McCallister!" She patted the bed, "C'mon Smoke." No response. She sat and gazed about the room. "Smoky!" she called. Panic filled her, and she sprang up, kneeled, and looked beneath the bed. She tore open the closet—no gray kitten. Grasping the knob of the French doors, she yanked them open. Cool evening air hit her face, but no Smoky appeared. Trying to keep her voice calm, she called, "Smoky . . . , Smoky . . . ," into the night.

A noise caused her to turn abruptly. There in the doorway from the hall stood Maggie, clutching the cat.

"Thank God." Laurel raced to her grandmother. "I was so worried."

Maggie gave Smoky to Laurel, walked to the desk, scratched words onto paper, and handed it to her granddaughter. Laurel read the words and laughed. "Yes, I did ask you to help with him. I forgot. Thank you. Maybe from now on you could leave me a note or something, so I don't worry. I don't know what I'd do without him," she said, hugging the furry, gray, yellow-eyed kitten.

With Smoky asleep at the bottom of the bed and her hair brushed, Laurel removed her bathrobe, preparing to slip into bed. Suddenly a noise outside her hall door drew her attention. No one knocked, but she heard footsteps and the rustle of paper. Walking over to the door, she noticed a slip of paper showing from beneath the door. Stooping, she picked it up and opened it.

Laurel:
Meet me at the rock in ten minutes. Urgent.

Ram

Laurel's hands shook with fright as she read the words. Why the rock? Was it a common meeting place? Jeremy had known about it from her story about the day she had become lost. How did Ram know she went there? *Meet him there at night? Never.* She calmly refolded the paper, slid it back under her door, and decided to pretend she'd never found it. *Perhaps that's what he'll think, too,* she assured herself. She tossed and turned for most of the night and once thought she heard someone outside her door. In the morning, the note was gone.

To avoid a confrontation with Ram, Laurel asked Maggie to bring her a breakfast tray. When Maggie's worried eyes pressed her for an excuse, Laurel merely pleaded laziness.

Maggie brought back a delightful-looking tray, set it on the desk, and disappeared out the French doors with Smoky. The aroma of fresh-perked coffee drew Laurel from the bed. She sat before the tray. Pouring her coffee, she noted how appetizing the food looked. Perhaps she should do this more often. Two eggs, a slice of ham, and delicious homemade bread sat on a plate beside a dish of fresh fruit. She enjoyed the breakfast in her room more than any she'd eaten sitting beside Ram Atwood.

After breakfast she spent the rest of the morning with her father, without telling him about Ram.

Laurel became restless at lunchtime and decided she needed fresh air and exercise. If Ram and the others were having their noon meal, she would be safe walking along the creek.

Passing the rock, pleasant memories of her first kiss enlivened her. She decided to walk farther than the rock, but not as far as the shanty or the place where they had discovered Dusty's body. Laurel found a peaceful area to sit and reflect. An odd-shaped tree afforded her a seat on its low, crooked branch. She sighed. It felt good to be outdoors, free and alive. Resting her head against the rough bark, she closed her eyes. Thoughts of Jeremy and her first kiss flooded her mind. She felt herself smile. Slowly, an unusual, uneasy feeling overcame Laurel. No longer did she feel alone, safe, and secure. Opening her eyes, she saw a figure looming over her. She jumped and gasped. How long had he been watching her?

"Ram, you frightened me!" she exclaimed breathlessly. "Why didn't you announce your presence?"

"Maybe I didn't want my presence known yet," he said boyishly.

Laurel prepared for flight.

"No. Don't go. I need to talk to you," he said.

Sitting back on her branch, she waited.

"I need an answer to one question, that's all," he stated simply.

She nodded.

"If I wanted to marry you, would I have a chance? Or have you pretty much selected Captain Grant?"

"You said one question. Which would you like an answer to?" she stalled.

"The first."

"I've not given marriage a thought. I've just found my new life and would like to get to know myself as I am." She studied him carefully and suddenly became brave. "May I ask *you* a question?"

"Sure."

"Why are you so concerned about my father's will, when he'll be around for quite some time? He's quite healthy."

"Who told you I was concerned?" he flared, his face distorted with anger.

"I overheard a conversation you had with your mother one day," she admitted.

He muttered an oath and slammed his fist down on the branch she sat upon, causing her to half jump and half slip off the limb.

Ram walked away from her with a brisk, serious gait. He turned a few feet away and pointed an angry finger at her. "You! I'm not through with you yet!" he spat and clumped away.

Laurel ran back to her room and paced. What would he do? Should she tell her father? Contact Jeremy? How could she decide?

Dressing for dinner, Laurel shivered at the thought of sitting beside Ram after their confrontation this afternoon. If she didn't appear, though, her father would worry.

Her reluctance nearly made her late, and Laurel entered the dining room last. Everyone awaited her: Ram, Ada, Maggie, and Angus all looked up as she entered, wearing a yellow chiffon dress, with a matching ribbon holding back her thick hair.

Everyone, including Ram, was congenial. Laurel wondered at the man's ability to act as if nothing had transpired between them. Was he sane?

After dinner, she resumed pacing in her room. Maggie had Smoky, so at least she didn't have to worry about disturbing him. Should she contact Jeremy? Opening the French doors, she stepped out and paced the balcony.

A knock on her hall door brought her back into the stuffy bedroom. Expecting Maggie or Ada, she was surprised to see Melita standing outside her door, weeping.

"Melita! Come in. What's wrong?" asked Laurel.

"You fool!" she spat, sniffling into her handkerchief. Closing the door, she fired questions at Laurel. "What did you tell Ram? And why did you let him see you and Jeremy kiss last night? Have you any idea what damage you've caused?"

"Ram was fine at dinner," Laurel said, at a loss for answers to her questions.

"Fine? He's furious! Have you any idea what that man is capable of or what he's capable of making me do?" she cried hysterically.

"Melita, calm down," Laurel soothed. "What do you mean capable of making you do?"

"Nothing. Just forget I was ever here tonight. Didn't Jeremy invite you to stay with him and Flora?"

"Yes, but I refused. I don't want to leave my father."

Melita took the handkerchief from her face and stared at Laurel. Her beautiful face was marred with red blotches from crying, and her crazed eyes looked blackened from smeared makeup. In her stress, she looked far different from the first time Laurel saw her. Could this be that same sophisticated, poised, educated woman whom she had envied? Laurel shivered.

Melita took a deep breath and practically whispered, "All

right, Laurel. I'll try talking with Ram. Maybe I can get him to change his mind. If I do, can I tell him you'll at least *consider* marrying him?"

Laurel hesitated, making a wry face.

"Laurel your *life* is in danger! At least *consider* it!" Melita snapped with such vehemence that Laurel instinctively backed up against the wall.

She and Ram are both crazy, Laurel thought, shivers running the length of her spine.

16

Just as Laurel put the finishing touches on her Sunday outfit Ada knocked on the door and announced that Jeremy had come for her. She had decided to wear a light-blue cotton, such as the other, simple, friendlier women wore. She didn't need to impress anyone with her rich clothes. Besides, the cotton was cooler and more comfortable. Laurel felt better in the simple dress, more herself. Placing a bonnet on her auburn hair, she pinched her cheeks and walked toward the living room to meet Captain Grant.

Jeremy smiled when she appeared. "You look beautiful." He opened the front door and helped her into the wagon. "The dress matches your eyes. Laurel, I don't think I've ever seen you look prettier—except maybe that first day, in your breeches, flannel shirt, and floppy hat."

She gave him a sideways glance, and they both laughed as the wagon started down the driveway. Laurel turned back toward the house in time to see Ram standing in front of the stable, staring after them.

The couple picked up Flora and continued on to church. Afterward they enjoyed a delicious meal at the Grant home. Flora, her usual bubbling self, seemed especially pleased that Laurel and Jeremy were not only getting along, but actually enjoying each other's company.

Just before dark, Laurel and Jeremy began their trip back to the ranch. Flora had baked a chocolate cake for the McCallisters, and Laurel held it on her lap.

Laurel confided to Jeremy the details of her latest visit from Melita and her concern for the stress the girl seemed to be under. Jeremy stopped the wagon.

"There's something I need to explain, Laurel," he said. "Melita and I. . . ." He looked at her apologetically.

"You don't need to explain . . . ," she began.

"But I do. Please. I've known Melita since we were kids. She's a beautiful girl, and I was flattered by her attention. I admit I didn't realize she was using me, but I didn't love her and couldn't set a wedding date. Dusty mistrusted her all along. He was an excellent judge of people." Jeremy looked heavenward. "God bless him."

"That reminds me," said Laurel. "During Dusty's memorial service the preacher said something I'm curious about. How does he or anyone else know Dusty's in heaven? Don't we all have to wait and be judged?"

"Some people believe that's how it will be. However, the Bible says in John 5:24 'Verily, verily, I say unto you, He that heareth my word, and believeth on him that sent me, hath everlasting life, and shall not come into condemnation; but is passed from death unto life.' "

"And God said those words?" she asked.

"Yes, He inspired men like John to write those words. You know, He put the words in his head."

Laurel thought for several seconds. "Jeremy, I must get my father to church with us."

"Pray for him."

"Why?" she asked in alarm. "Is he ill?"

Jeremy laughed. "No, I mean pray that he'll go to church with you."

A thoughtful smile curved her mouth. "I will."

He picked up the reins and urged the horses forward. When they reached the house, he walked her to the door. Taking care not to crush the cake, he kissed her good night.

"Don't forget, if you need me, tell Maggie; she knows how to reach me. Manuel is still hanging around. I haven't left you entirely on your own."

Going straight to her room, after delivering the cake to the kitchen, Laurel took the large Bible from the night stand. She paged and paged until she found John 5:24, read the words slowly, and wondered how Jeremy had remembered them exactly. Did Maggie know about this?

Walking down the hall, she knocked softly on Maggie's door. The door opened a crack, and two noses poked out, one near the floor and very gray, the other Maggie's.

Laurel laughed. "Hello, you two! I've come for a visit." She scooped up Smoky as Maggie pulled her inside. Kissing Smoky's head, she let him down and pushed the Bible under Maggie's nose. "Read this verse, John 5:24."

Maggie took the book to her rocking chair, sat beneath a bright floor lamp, and read the words. She then looked at Laurel with questioning eyes.

"God said that!" Laurel exclaimed. "That's how Jeremy and the people in his church know Dusty is in heaven. Isn't that wonderful to *know* you're going to heaven, without a doubt?"

Maggie smiled knowingly, then flipped back a few pages

and pointed to a verse someone had circled. Maggie urged her to read it. " 'For God so loved the world, that he gave his only begotten Son, that whosoever believeth in him should not perish, but have everlasting life' (John 3:16)."

Laurel hugged her grandmother. "Oh, Gram, I'm so glad you know this, too. Now no matter what happens to either of us, we'll never be separated again."

Maggie smiled with tearing eyes and returned her hug.

"Gram, does Father know these things?"

Maggie sobered and shook her head. She took a pencil and wrote on a paper, *He used to, before your mother died.*

"Will you help me pray for him?" she asked earnestly.

Maggie smiled, wiping away a stray tear. She nodded.

"I'll take Smoky back to my room," Laurel announced, picking up the kitten. "Good night. See you at breakfast."

Back in her room, Laurel brushed her hair and thought about all the things that had transpired this day. A noise called her attention to the French doors. Smoky scratched at the glass.

"Do you need to go out?"

"Meo-o-w." Smoky rubbed his body against the glass and looked up at her expectantly.

"Okay, but you come right back in when I call you." She opened the door, and he squeezed through before she even had it opened all the way. "Silly fellow!" She laughed.

Laurel fished in the drawer for her pink nightgown and matching bathrobe. She removed her clothing and donned the nightclothes. After washing in the basin, she started to take the sudsy bowl out onto the balcony to toss, when Smoky dashed in, whizzing between her legs and nearly caused her to drop the water. She set down the basin and followed him under the bed. What did she smell? What had Smoky gotten himself into?

Pulling the frightened kitten out from under the bed, by his hind feet, she gagged.

"Smoky, where were you? Did you knock over someone's lantern or lamp? You reek of kerosene. Ugh! It's a good thing I didn't dump my bathwater!"

Dunking the errant kitten into the sudsy water, and covering him with soap she commented, "You look mighty puny without all your fluffy hair! That's the best I can do with such a small amount of water. Tomorrow you'll get a regular bath. This just means you and I can share a room tonight!"

Towel drying the trembling gray cat, she removed as much wetness as possible from his fur. After rolling on the floor several minutes, a damp Smoky finally snuggled up beside Laurel. Both slept soundly.

Laurel awoke to a strange, frantic scratching noise. Sitting straight up from a sound sleep, she looked around the moonlit room. Simultaneously three things struck her: Smoky's scratching at the door and crying, an odd smell, and the fogginess that filled the room. Her heart pounded in alarm.

Springing from the bed, Laurel tried to open the French doors, but they seemed stuck. Gaining strength from her anxiety, she forced open the door with every bit of muscle she had and noticed that someone had wedged the porch chair beneath the doorknob. *Why? Who?* But she had no time for questions.

As Smoky ran off into the night, she turned back toward the hall door and coughed. A crackling sound made her realize the smell came from a fire! Laurel hesitated. She could run to safety as Smoky had done, but what about the rest of the household? When she opened her bedroom door to the hall, heat and thick smoke hit her face, temporarily taking her breath away. She slammed the door shut. How could she reach her father and Maggie? Were they aware of the danger?

Opening the door again, she yelled, "Help, fire!" slammed it shut quickly, and ran for the balcony. Thick smoke filled the room now, and she slowed to feel her way, coughing and gagging. She reached the French doors just as a dark figure burst into the room.

"Laurel! Are you all right?"

"Jeremy! Thank God it's you!"

He hugged her to him briefly. "C'mon, out on the balcony," he ordered.

"I can't. What about my father and Maggie?"

"Do what I say quickly, so I can get them, too!" he commanded. "Run to the stable and stay there until I come for you." She obeyed.

Though dark, and dreary, at least the stable provided fresh air and safety. Flames from the burning house cast an eerie orange glow on the barn. Laurel knelt in the straw and prayed as she'd never prayed before.

Back on her feet, she decided she had to know what was happening. She left the barn and merely stood in front of it. Fiery teeth bit at the ranch home, devouring it with a sinister roar. Had Jeremy reached her father? Maggie? What about Ram and Ada?

Suddenly a figure broke through the haze. Jeremy! He carried someone. As they drew closer she could see it was her father. Jeremy laid him down at Laurel's feet and ran back toward the house. "I'm going for Maggie," he yelled.

"Be careful, Jeremy!" she called after him.

"Are you all right, Father?" She stooped, raising his head with one hand.

He coughed. "Fine, thanks to your friend Jeremy. That's two I owe him now!"

"Do you know where the rest are?"

"No. I pointed out Maggie's room to Jeremy. Hope he gets to her on time; the smoke's pretty thick in there."

Seconds later, Jeremy appeared with another bundle: Maggie.

"I can't go in for anyone else. The whole place is ablaze! The walls are caving in, and we barely made it out. Help me with Maggie; she isn't breathing."

Angus, Jeremy, and Laurel all took turns trying to get Maggie to respond. They breathed into her mouth, they sat her up and slapped her back, to no avail. Jeremy felt for her pulse and shook his head sadly.

"No!" Laurel screamed. "Gram! Wake up, Gram! Don't be dead! Please, don't be dead!"

Jeremy pulled her away. "It's too late, Laurel. She was too old for that smoke. She didn't suffer, just never woke from her restful sleep."

Laurel sobbed, "But I'll miss her terribly!"

"We all will," said Angus sadly.

Wiping her tears, Laurel brightened somewhat. "She knew your Bible verse, Jeremy, and she showed me another one. I know she's in heaven with Dusty!"

Jeremy held her in his arms. "I know it, too, Laurel." He led her over to her father. While they stood watching the inferno, Jeremy carried Maggie into the barn and laid her upon the straw.

When he returned, Angus slapped Jeremy's back. "My boy, you saved our lives! How can I ever thank you?"

"When this is all over, I may give you the opportunity, sir."

"What about Ada?" Angus suddenly cried.

"I tried, sir . . . ," Jeremy began. "Her wing of the house went ablaze first—There was no way . . . ," he faltered again. "I'm sorry."

Tears rolled down Angus's face. "She was a fine woman. I'll miss her."

"We'll *all* miss her. What a horrid thing to happen."

Laurel silently shook her head then perked up and addressed Jeremy, "Jeremy, what made you come here tonight? How did you know about the fire?"

"Manuel came for me. He saw something suspicious and ran for me. By the time I arrived, the flames were already beginning to engulf the house."

"What did Manuel see?" Laurel asked.

"We'll discuss it later," he said with a warning glance.

Laurel turned to Jeremy. "Where's my grandmother?"

Jeremy signaled toward the barn.

"May I say good-bye to her?"

"Are you sure you can handle it?" Concern filled his eyes.

"Now that I know she's with Dusty, I think I can."

Laurel walked into the barn and stared at the sight before her. Maggie lay peacefully upon the straw, and Smoky had curled up across her neck, with his face resting on hers. He, too, was saying his farewells.

Laurel kissed her grandmother's face. "See you in heaven, Gram. Say hello to Dusty for us, and tell him we miss him, too. I won't cry anymore for you, because we'll all be together again one day. Won't that be fun? See you!" Laurel kissed Maggie again and picked up Smoky.

"Oh, Gram!" Laurel exclaimed. "The Tatums told me that in heaven our bodies will be perfect. You'll be able to talk! You're probably talking right this minute to Dusty!"

Hearing a chuckle, Laurel looked up. "Jeremy! How long have you been there?"

"Not long enough. I'm afraid I probably missed the best funeral message of all time!" He wrapped a blanket around her. She'd forgotten she still wore only the pink nightgown. "I'm taking you and your father to our house."

Jeremy handed Laurel up onto the wagon. Her father lay in the back, beneath a blanket, and Jeremy gave him Smoky to hold.

Before Jeremy started the horses, he and Laurel stared at the destroyed ranch. Flames still leapt up here and there, and smoke smoldered above some blackened objects.

"I'm sorry, Laurel. Your home is gone."

She thought a moment, then brightened. "We'll build another."

17

Angus held his cane in one hand and Laurel's arm in the other as he stepped up the few steps into the schoolhouse-church. Jeremy and Flora followed. As they found seats, Angus looked about uncomfortably. "The roof didn't cave in," he whispered to Laurel.

She smiled. "You aren't sorry you came?"

"No, I'm glad I decided to come. I have much to be thankful for, and it took what happened this week to wake me up. I want to thank God personally."

"But you could have done that at home," she reminded.

"Yes, I could have. Always was a prayin' man until. . . . Anyway, I wanted to come because I knew you wanted me to and to show God just how grateful I am. I'm going to come every week; I'll put God back into my life."

Laurel merely smiled as the service began.

After the sermon, the Reverend Billy Childs asked the congregation if anyone had anything special to add to the service. An old man stood. "I thank the Lord for answer to prayer. My wife took sick with a high fever. I spent a great deal of time in prayer, and this morning her fever was gone."

Several people "oh-ed and ah-ed," and a few said, "Praise be."

Others acknowledged God working in their lives. Then much to Laurel's surprise, Angus stood and faced the congregation. "God answered my prayer before I asked!" he nearly shouted. Once he had everyone's rapt attention, he continued, more calmly, "Almost twenty years ago, my wife was killed in an Indian raid right here in Fort Worth. My daughter was taken by these Comanche, and I hadn't seen or heard from her until about a month ago. During that whole time I never prayed, because I stubbornly blamed God and pouted because I hadn't gotten my way. I felt sorry for myself."

Angus gazed at his audience. "Yet deep within me I felt myself crying out to Him. I tried to deny it, but now know I must have been praying with the part of me that didn't know I'd quit Him." He laughed. "Quit God! As if that were possible. How can someone quit God? Once you know Him, as I did, and He is a central figure in your life, there is no quitting Him. The human part of you, perhaps, shuts Him out, but your soul can never quit Him. Deep within He remains your God, forever. And the wonderful part of it is, despite everything. . . ." Angus's voice cracked with emotion, and his eyes filled. "Despite everything, He never quits you."

A sudden stirring rustled through the audience as handkerchiefs were put to use, and people murmured in agreement.

"I came here today to thank God for several things. This week He spared my worthless life, spared the life of my precious daughter, whom I'm just getting acquainted with, and gave me the opportunity to share this with you. Let me finish by saying, if you know someone who's been reared in God and strayed, don't fret. Just pray. That person's spirit is still with God, and he or she needs your prayers, not your preaching."

Angus dabbed his eyes and sat down.

Oh the way to the wagon, after the service, several people came to Angus and thanked him for sharing his story. Jeremy patted his back. "I'm proud of you," he said.

"I still owe you, Son."

"Yes, and I plan to collect soon." Jeremy laughed.

Flora outdid herself with a delicious dinner, but Jeremy was called away during the meal by an army messenger. While she served coffee in the living room, Flora worried about Jeremy's errand. "I wonder what's happening now. Do you suppose he has to return to Fort Sill?"

"Surely they'll let him stay for the funeral, won't they?" Laurel asked.

"Maggie's is tomorrow and Ada's, Tuesday. I don't expect they'd call him back before that," said Flora.

"Has anyone seen Ram or Melita since the fire?" Angus wondered.

"No one," Flora and Laurel chorused.

"Now, Angus," Flora shook her finger at him. "I want you to know that you and Laurel are welcome here as long as you wish. If you decide to rebuild, you can stay here until you finish—no matter how long it takes. We love having you both."

"That's kind of you," said Angus. "We are indeed fortunate to have friends like you and Jeremy."

A slamming door brought Flora to attention. "Is that you, Jeremy?" she called. "We're in the living room."

Jeremy entered with a pale face.

"Jeremy! What is it?"

Angus and Laurel merely stared.

Jeremy sat down beside Laurel on the sofa. He gazed at each of them for several seconds. "I don't know how to tell you this."

"What?" begged Flora. "What has happened now?"

Jeremy played with his hands nervously. "The army men I brought back with me from Fort Sill have been investigating the fire and Ram's criminal actions. They think they've found Melita and Ram and need me to identify them."

"Identify them?" Angus, Laurel, and Flora said at once.

Jeremy sighed. "It seems that two bodies have been found in the old shanty—a man and a woman. They seem to be quite dead. It appears to be murder-suicide. The woman had the gun in her hand. The man was shot through the temple; the woman through the chest."

"Dear God!" breathed Flora, holding her own chest.

"And they think," said Laurel, "that she—"

Jeremy nodded.

"They were both acting crazy toward the end . . . ," Laurel offered.

"We'll never know exactly what happened," said Jeremy, "but that's how it looks. They also found a considerable amount of kerosene on Melita's clothing, and her skirt was scorched. The army men think the shooting took place just hours after the fire, and we had no way of knowing until now."

Laurel's head swung quickly toward Jeremy. "You never *did* tell us exactly what Manuel said that made you come to the ranch the night of the fire."

"Manuel ran all the way to our house, and by the time I

realized what he was blabbering about in half Spanish and half English, I feared being too late."

"How do you think I felt," added Flora, "left here alone to wonder?"

"What did Manuel see?" Laurel asked.

"Manuel saw Melita pouring something all around the house. When I asked him what she poured, he shrugged and said something that smelled like a lamp."

Laurel shook her head. "But why would Melita set the house on fire? Last time I talked to her, she didn't want *anyone* to die."

"Maybe Ram told her to do it. If he made her think she had to choose between losing him to you and taking your life, in her state of mind, burning the house might have seemed the best thing to do."

"But then Ram would have had to order his own mother's death." Laurel objected. "*She* was in the house, too."

"Looks like Ram didn't intend to share his wealth with anyone." Jeremy shrugged. "Perhaps Ada was not supposed to be there, or one of the army men suggested that perhaps Melita only poured kerosene on your wing of the house. The wind was blowing toward Ada's wing, which is a detail Melita and Ram may not have considered."

"God rest their troubled souls," murmured Flora.

Jeremy had to return to Fort Sill for his final year of duty, and Laurel wrote him daily. How she missed him! Her love grew by leaps and bounds now that the troubled waters had stilled. Remarkably, she and Angus thrived under Flora's attention, and everyone got along wonderfully. Flora became the mother Laurel never had. Under her tutelage, Laurel learned to knit, crochet, bake bread and other luscious things, and to cook almost as well as Mrs. Grant herself. Yet they all missed Jeremy.

At Christmas, much to the joy of everyone, Jeremy came home for two weeks. Laurel cooked the festive Christmas dinner as a surprise gift to him.

After dinner Jeremy addressed Angus McCallister, "Angus, you claim you owe me because I brought your daughter back and saved your life. Remember I said one day I'd ask to have the deeds returned?"

"I do, and I shall honor that promise," said Angus proudly.

"Then come with me to the study, for I am ready for my favor." Jeremy walked to the study; Angus followed, and he closed the door behind them.

"What do you suppose that's about?" asked Laurel. "I can't believe Jeremy is going to ask Father to return a favor!"

Flora smiled, knowingly. "I hope it's what I think it is."

"You know?"

"No, just hoping, praying, and knowing my son."

"They're coming out already. That didn't take long," remarked Laurel.

"Laurel, may I see you in the study?" Jeremy asked.

"Sure," she replied, following him.

When the door was closed, he took her into his arms. "Laurel, I've missed you," he whispered huskily.

She looked up into his eyes and admitted, "I've also missed you."

"I've asked your father for one favor, and he has granted it, but only if you agree."

"I—agree?" she repeated.

"Yes. Will you marry me?"

"Oh-h! *That's* the favor? You asked for my hand?"

"Yes. What is your answer?"

She studied him. "Well, that depends."

"Depends?"

"What will you do for a living? Surely you aren't going to

stay in the army and be far away forever? And do you want children? If so how many? Will you allow me as many cats as I choose? Most important, do you love me—and will you forever?"

Jeremy laughed. "I wondered when you'd get to the important part. In answer to your first question, I plan to leave the army in six months. Your father has offered me the job of running his ranch, and I've accepted. I'd like as many children as you want, preferably half a dozen. As to cats, I set a limit of two in the house, but you may have as many as you please outdoors. And yes, I love you more than I've ever loved anything or anyone, and I know that love will grow. Will you say yes?"

"There is one other thing I need to know. What about my father? Will I always be able to be near him?"

"I promise."

"My life so far as Laurel McCallister hasn't been such a success. I'm anxious to try as Laurel Grant." She looked up at him with dreamy eyes. "Yes, I'll marry you."

Six months later, Angus and Laurel again attended church, only the day was a Saturday. The bell that usually called children to class rang loudly, and sun poured over the little schoolhouse-church, spilling through the windows and streaking the interior with its beams. Amid the largest patch of rays stood Angus and Jeremy, nervously waiting by the makeshift altar, Reverend Billy Childs before them.

As music sounded, two brides appeared—one young with auburn hair and the other wearing a grin that stretched from ear to ear. Each took her place beside her prospective husband. Flora tucked her arm beneath Angus's, while Laurel placed a hand on Jeremy's sleeve.

Following vows and kisses, the couples received the

congratulations of their well-wishers and happily hopped into the buckboard. A short ride brought their new home in view. Where the charred remains of a one-story ranch once lay, stood a white, two-story home, with pillars, French doors, and floor-to-ceiling windows.

Flora and Angus headed for the wing on the east side of the house, while Laurel and Jeremy stood outside and watched the sun set over theirs.

"You and Father did a splendid job on the house, Jeremy. It's beautiful. I cannot believe I've come from a drafty tepee to this magnificent home."

His arm tightened about her. "We combined our resources to help us all make a new life together, with God."

Laurel smiled up at her beloved husband, "God has been good. He's answered my prayers before I've asked, just by knowing me and what I needed. I've found my father and the most wonderful husband."

Squeezing her husband's hand, she gazed up at him and asked, "Do you think Grandmother and Dusty can see our happiness?"

Jeremy chuckled. "They may have even put in a good word for us!"

Laughing, hand in hand, a gray cat prancing behind them, the couple walked up the path to their new home and new life.